LADIES IN THE PARLOR

LADIES IN THE PARLOR
by
Jim Tully

UNDERWORLD AMUSEMENTS
Baltimore

COPYRIGHT, 1935, BY
JIM TULLY

ISBN13 - 9780983031437
ISBN- 0-9830314-3-6

This edition edited by Underworld Amusements for *JimTully.net*
Visit the website for information on Tully and his work.
Available for purchase at select retailers.
www.UnderworldAmusements.com

Typsetting and design by Kevin I. Slaughter
Cover photography by CatFight!
www.CatFightPhotography.com

To
W. D. GREET
GEORGE STAHLMAN
AND
WALTER WINCHELL
COMPANIONS

"*Down the roadway in the dusk,*
Where the shapes of hunger wander
And the fugitives of pain go by."

A philosophy undoubtedly perverse has induced me to believe that good and evil, pleasure and sorrow, beauty and ugliness, reason and folly, are blended, one into thy other, by shades as indiscernible as those on the neck of a dove.

ERNEST RENAN

Chapter 1

Leora Blair was the oldest of nine brothers and sisters. Her home was on the Ohio River.

Her mother had flat breasts and a tired expression. Her eyes were bleared, her voice whined. She always wore a calico dress buttoned down the front.

Leora's father was a shambling man with narrow, stooped shoulders, a coconut head, and a red, bulbous nose. One eye was smaller and lower than the other. His high cheek-bones seemed ready to break out of the skin.

When he became angry at his wife, he would pull his tobacco-stained mustache, and scream, "God Almighty, every time I hang my pants on the bed, you git knocked up." The mother, with nine bits of evidence all around her, would make no comment.

Bill Blair worked from seven at night till seven each morning of the week in the round-house of a railroad.

He would steal several hours' sleep each night. This gave him many waking hours at home, over which he ruled with hate. His wages were seventy-five dollars a month and his duties were to clean the engines.

His nine children dreaded his presence in the house. All were happier when he started for work each night.

Leora Blair early learned to hate and avoid him.

Her eyes were vivid and blue. Her hair was deep brown, wavy, and tinged with auburn.

Beautiful early, it was hard to imagine her the child of such parents.

One afternoon her brother was an hour late in returning from an errand for his father. The parent met the boy on the porch and whipped him severely. Rebelling at last, the boy turned suddenly, knocked his father down, and kicked him in the ribs, calling him a Goddamned, red-nosed son-of-a-bitch.

Still in a rage, the boy left the home. Meeting Leora at the gate, he said quickly, "Good-bye, Sis—I'm on my way."

Leora watched him hurry in the direction of the river and for the first and only time in her childhood, she had a feeling of loneliness for him. She stepped onto the porch just as her father was crawling into the house. "Go call your mother," he yelled at her.

The girl looked at him.

"You God-damned brat, call your mother," her father shook his fist.

The mother heard him yelling and dragged her feet from the back yard.

"Leora, run and git some hot water for your father." Leora stood still.

The mother glanced at her defiant daughter and went for the water.

The father was, by this time, in a pine rocking chair. He glared at his daughter.

"God'll punish you," he said.

Hate welled in her eyes.

Her father clutched at his side; then rushed and grabbed Leora. She pounded at him and buried her teeth in his wrist. He released his grip with a moan, screaming, "You God-damn little spitfire."

Leora slammed the door and was gone.

The mother went to her husband and asked plaintively, "What'll we ever do with that child?"

"We'll send her to the reform school," said the father, "She ain't fit to live in a decent home."

The mother made no answer.

A few weeks later, the father caught Leora lightly caressing a neighbor boy.

After she had struggled until exhausted, he beat her unmercifully.

"I'll teach her she can't disgrace the Blairs," he shouted to his wife, who came running toward them.

For a moment her scrawny hands opened and shut like angry talons, as she glared at her husband. "If you touch her agin, I'll kill you—you, and your talk about disgracin' the God-damned Blairs."

He stood, frightened before the rage of his wife.

Leora went to her mother's side. Her arm went round the child. Her hand patted its shoulder.

"What'd you beat her for?"

"For carryin's on, that's what," he answered sullenly.

"It's too bad," shouted the mother, "that Leora can't put her arm around a neighbor boy."

"Don't, Mother," said Leora, "it's the last time—he'll never beat me no more."

With her arm still around the child, they walked to the house.

That night the mother soothed her child's body with witch-hazel. Stopping for a second in her rubbing, she gazed at the lovely body of her daughter, just beginning to bud.

"Mother," said the girl, "I hate every hair in his head, and I'll run away, too."

"Please don't," pleaded the mother, "what'll I do without both you an' Buddy?" She sobbed, "Promise me you won't leave."

It was some time before Leora said, "All right."

"Besides," said the mother, "you mustn't hate, Leora; it'll get you nowheres."

"Well, love ain't got you no place," returned the child.

After Leora was asleep, the mother lay by the child's bed a long time and watched her body twitch.

Finally, Leora sighed in deep slumber. The tired, flat-breasted mother rose, looked down at her, and said softly to herself, "Lord, she's purty," then knelt by the bedside and held the child's hand.

Doors slammed as the other children entered the house. Still the mother sat by the child.

At last she pulled the quilt over the young breasts, just beginning to swell.

Standing erect, she rubbed her own flat breasts and left the room. She dragged herself to the kitchen, cleared the dirty dishes from the oil-cloth covered table and piled them in a dishpan. Going to the well, she pumped a bucket of water, poured it over the dishes to "let 'em soak till morning." Then, without undressing, she fell, exhausted, across her unmade bed.

Chapter 2

Leora awoke early. Her aching body would not let her sleep. More distinctly than ever she heard the deep breathing of her brothers and sisters and the restless rolling of her mother.

She could hear the whistle of a boat on the river. "Maybe the 'River Queen' coming from Cincinnati," she thought.

She went to the small window at the gabled end of the small pine house and gazed across the river. People were leaving a large well-lit boat. She sat very still for a long time.

The most pleasant hours of her childhood had been spent in watching the boats go up and down the river.

Several times each summer a showboat would stop at the foot of Fulton Street.

She would often loiter about the boat with her cousin, Alice Tracy, who was three years older than herself.

Her aunt would take Alice and herself to see the plays on the boat.

Alice had later joined a company on a showboat, and was now in Chicago.

In spite of her numerous brothers and sisters, Leora's life had often been solitary in the town, which was laid out like a checkerboard, the poorer people living in small pine houses "over the tracks." All the houses were built alike on the street where Leora lived. A stranger was not able to tell them apart.

The town was a railroad division point. It literally lived "on the railroad." Engineers and conductors were at the top of the social scale. Dates were set by "pay days." They came once a month. A picnic, for instance, would not be held too long after pay day. A young man, beginning as a railroader, and who joined a lodge, married on credit and settled down to a life of debt, was highly considered in the town.

There was a woods to the rear of the Blair home, known as Hardy's Grove. It was used as a picnic ground during the summer. A creek ran at one edge of it toward the river. Comprising ten acres, a wagon road and paths led to the center where a raised platform had been built. Here, for a period dating before the Civil War, the politicians of their little day had expounded. Large elms, beeches, and sycamores lined each side of the creek. Their branches intertwined overhead. Through them the sun dappled the water with shadow.

Here Leora had played from childhood. Her brother had made a swing under a long sycamore branch, which she used frequently.

Gypsies came regularly to the center of Hardy's Grove and traded horses with the natives, while their women told fortunes.

They would camp along the creek for several days, and travel on as mysteriously as they came. They never failed to fill Leora with wonder. Their vari-colored clothes and the freedom of their lives made her overlook the filth of which her aunt complained.

Though the men cheated the natives when they traded horses, the women made friends with the children by telling them pleasant fortunes and only charging them twenty-five cents.

One had held Leora's hand and told her a fortune that a queen might envy. The children laughed, while her aunt wondered if it would "turn out true."

Her aunt lived across the grove. She was Leora's father's sister, and was known in the town as Red Moll because of her fondness for bright red dresses.

Her house of seven rooms and one story was in the front of a hickory woods. Living with her were young women known as "boarders." It was visited often by men, and, as a consequence, Red Moll was spurned in the town. Whether or not she cared, no one knew. She owned the house. It was out of the jurisdiction of the town.

She did not like her brother, but was fond of his wife and children. If Mrs. Blair knew of her sister-in-law's reputation, she accepted it with the resignation with which she had given birth to her children.

While some of the women in the town wondered if part of their husbands' money had not gone to the girls at Red Moll's, she was unmolested in the town. The girls at her house came and went, and some preferred to "rest up" at Red Moll's for months at a time.

Red Moll had one gold tooth in the center of her mouth. Her lips were thin, her mouth small. The gold tooth marred an otherwise attractive smile. It was called a "Cincinnati tooth" and was rare in the town. Engineers and the more prosperous citizens went to Cincinnati to have dental work done.

Red Moll was slender, with a quick step and graceful carriage. If any man other than her husband, long ago killed in a wreck, had been in her life, that also was a secret.

As usual in such a town, the men talked about the public women they knew. Evidently no one had known Red Moll intimately. It was said once that she had gone away with a leading carriage manufacturer to Cincinnati, and that later he had paid the mortgage on her home, and died. Red Moll did not attend the funeral, and never mentioned his name.

Leora had heard considerable about her aunt through indirect gossip. But, like her aunt, indifferent and silent by nature, it concerned her not at all.

Each year Red Moll's yard was full of red geraniums. Nasturtiums and morning-glories climbed over her paling fence, and grape-vines over a latticed pergola that half-filled the back yard, and covered the boardwalk that led to the hickory grove.

Her home was gaudily furnished with red plush chairs and couches. Her own room was simple as a nun's. In one corner was a plaster statue of the Blessed Virgin in a glass case.

On the center table was a booklet showing scenes of the World's Fair at St. Louis. Where it came from, Red Moll had forgotten. Near it was a small vase labeled NIAGARA FALLS. In the living-room was a crude painting advertising "Green River Whisky." An old Negro leaned on a mule. To its saddle was strapped a jug of liquor. Beneath were the words, "THEY WERE BRED IN OLD KENTUCKY."

Four statues of nude women, done in plaster, were on the mantelpiece. Several scenes from the Passion Play hung on the wall near by.

A large oil lamp, with a red-flowered shade, was on a yellow oak table. Black dots, supposed to be hummingbirds, flew among the flowers. It was really a kerosene lamp, but Red Moll had it wired for electricity. She would turn the light on at dusk and watch the birds sip at the flowers. Each year she bought cheap calendars and hung them on the walls of the different rooms. When merchants gave her a pictured calendar she liked, she would keep it for years, taking the months from a less pretty calendar and attaching them to it.

She had an immense "grandfather's clock." It was one of the few in the town. It stood in the hallway, in a space far too small for it. It chimed the hours away in music. A drunken railroader had once broken the glass at the bottom. He offered to pay Red Moll for the damage. She refused to accept the money, but never allowed him to come to her house again. Later she had a bright brass rail placed in front of the clock.

Whenever traveling salesmen "wanted a woman," they were sent to Red Moll's house. Often she would "furnish a girl" who would call at the hotel. Returning, she would give Red Moll half her earnings.

While none of these dealings ever made her rich, they kept her from becoming too poor. Red Moll was a woman through whose hands money went like sand. She had but one fear, that of losing her home. That fear made her pay her taxes regularly and manipulate money in every manner possible to keep the home from being mortgaged.

Red Moll never talked of this fear. But those who saw her place pots of geraniums in her "hot room" each fall knew how much she loved her home.

Whenever a child was born in the Blair home, Red Moll would go and help, then leave quietly, without comment. The children learned to lean upon her.

When Leora was eleven, she was allowed to stay all night with Alice. From then on, she came and went whenever in the mood.

Leora spent many hours out-of-doors with Red Moll, who knew the name and nature of every tree in Hardy's Grove.

When Alice was gone, Leora remained longer with her aunt at each visit. Woman and girl would talk of Alice quietly.

"She'll get along—she's that kind," Alice's mother once said to Leora.

Alice wrote to them each week. They would read the letters together.

In one letter, Alice begged her mother to visit Chicago.

"You write to her, Leora," said the mother, "and tell her I'm here whenever she wants to see me."

Chicago seemed far away to Leora. It was nearly four hundred miles.

She had missed Alice and the picnics which they had together at Hardy's Grove.

For many minutes she thought of her aunt and Alice, while the lights became dim on the boat, and the dying moon turned the river into gold.

A breeze stirred and chilled her body. She pulled her nightgown more closely about her, and wondered about her brother. Buddy had gone away so often. It might be this was the last time. Leora wished she were a boy. Her brother had said to her, "You ought to get out of this, Sis. I'm goin' to."

But how to get out of it—and what to do? Sadly Leora remembered she had promised her mother to stay.

The bed squeaked as her mother rolled over. The odor of nine bodies rushed by Leora, like ill-smelling ghosts, anxious to get out of the window. Fastidious about her body to the verge of mania, Leora had shuddered for years at the close proximity of all her family.

Leora went to the bed for her clothes. Her body ached as she put them on. A fierce sense of loneliness came over her. Rebellion nearly choked her. Stealthily she went down the stairs and into the yard with the burnt brown grass.

She walked about the town, with only the echo of her footsteps for company.

A light was still shining in one house a few blocks from her own. Leora stood in front of it for several moments. The curtains were far up. Moving about inside was Dr. Jonas Farway. He was about thirty-five, with heavy shoulders, a large head, and jaws so heavy they protruded at the sides.

Of medium height, he looked more the athlete than the doctor, though he was popular with all the poorer families along the river.

The girl had often seen him and had heard his name for at least five years. Some months before he had been in her house. Her mother had fallen down stairs and wrenched her ankle. At that time Leora had stood near the bed, by the doctor's side. When leaving he put an arm about her and held her against him for a moment, so taut that it hurt her breasts. Though it was done playfully, Leora understood.

Her body tingled now as she watched him.

Suddenly the light went out. Leora walked slowly home and lay upon her bed without undressing. Unable to sleep, she stared upward in the dark until dawn. Restless, she rose and sat on the porch until the factory whistles blew at seven.

A clatter arose in the house. The family was getting up.

Her father would soon be home. She had avoided him before. Now she sat quite still. Seeing him coming, she went into the house and took a pair of sharp scissors from the sewing machine drawer and returned to her chair on the porch.

When Blair entered the yard, rattling his tin dinner bucket, he looked in surprise at Leora and half sneered, "You here?"

"Yes, I'm here; I couldn't sleep from your beating."

He started toward her and stopped suddenly, seeing the scissors in her hand.

"If you ever lay a dirty hand on me again," she cried, "I'll stab you—and if I don't while you're doin' it, I'll stab you while you sleep. You ain't goin' to run me away like you did my brother."

The startled father asked, "Ain't he back yet?"

"No, and I don't think he's coming back this time."

"He's like you," said the father, "he belongs in the reform school."

"Nobody thinks so but you. You're so mean you hate your shadow. He's a good boy; you just pounded him till he's like a beaten-up dog, and damn you, you'll suffer for it. Now I want to tell you, I'm not running away and I'm not going to the reform school, and if you send me, I'll run away and sneak in the house and stab you. I want you to let me alone. You may be stronger'n me, but that's no sign you can scare me."

The mother came to the porch.

"You hear this, Ma?" asked the father.

The flat-breasted woman stood erect. "Yes, I heard it and all I'm sayin' is—she's right. God never gave no man the right to beat Leora's nice body till it's black and blue'. You drove my boy away—for he ain't in his bed."

The mother trembled and sobbed with new-found courage.

The other children gathered about and stared at Leora.

"Take Ma inside," she said, "And you, Sally, go get us some breakfast."

The father stared after the mother as the children helped her, still sobbing, inside the house.

"This is a purty thing to come home to." He stepped toward the porch.

"It's what you deserve," the girl said.

"If you don't put up them scissors, I'll call the police."

The girl sneered, "You beat us up, and if we fight back, you call the cops." She stepped forward. "Go ahead and call them. I'll tell them what you did to Buddy, and show them what you did to me. We take your beatings because we're proud, but I'm not proud no more—and I want you to let us alone—every one of us."

The words stunned the father.

"All right," he said.

The girl stepped on the burnt lawn. The father went into the house.

Breakfast was eaten in silence. The meal finished, Sally rose and asked, half to herself, "I wonder where Buddy is."

The children looked at Leora, then at the father. The mother left the table, sobbing. Leora and Sally went to comfort her.

Mrs. Blair had leaned on Leora more than on her other children. Leora, in turn, had mingled contempt and kindness for her. For years she had heard of her mother's girlhood and of her marriage.

"He was a handsome man then," her mother used to say. "No better looking man ever made love to a woman nowheres."

Leora, allowing her mother to dream, would make no comment.

She had suffered long with Blair, a failure at everything. After their marriage they had gone on their wedding trip in a prairie schooner to a homestead which Blair bad taken in the West.

She wore a calico dress of white, sprigged with pink roses. A large sunbonnet was drawn over her hair. It was then the shade of her beautiful daughter's.

For over three weeks they were on the way. The roads were drifted cattle trails. They did not talk much. When she became tired of gazing at the far horizon she would watch the wagon wheels turning in the sand.

She stayed in a sod house of two rooms with Blair for four years. Unusual in that section, it had a rough pine floor. In all that time she did not go near a town.

Bent by the wind, dusty weeds rattled in the yard.

To keep the rattlesnakes away from their home, barbed wire was laid on the ground at a safe distance from the house. Blair had explained to her that they would not crawl over anything sharp.

She heard a hissing sound one day. A rattlesnake was coiled in a corner. She ran out of the house and would not enter until Blair came home and killed the snake.

She was heavy with child at the time. The fear of losing the baby paralyzed her for days.

Mrs. Blair dreamed vaguely of better times to come, how or when, she did not know.

She would watch the storm clouds gather and disperse. Rain in would now and then splash on the hot earth and disappear. The cattle would moo contentedly and switch their tails as it fell upon them. Thoughts of escape would come to her. The child kicking in her womb made her brush them aside. Besides, a promise made before God was not to be lightly broken by her. If she did not love Blair, he was the only human creature she knew. She clung to him in desperation.

Her nearest neighbors were eight miles to the north, where a dozen cowboys were in charge of a cattle camp. The closest woman lived twelve miles to the south.

Each night, after their animal-like embraces, she would lie awake and listen to the wind in the sand-grass, or the mooing of the cattle roaming about in the dark.

The post office was in a small village thirty miles away. It made no difference. No one ever wrote to her.

She was alone when one baby was born. Blair had gone to the village.

The pains began to gripe her.

Hardly able to bear them, she dug her nails into her palms. Sweat stood on her forehead. In agony, she tore the clothes from her body. She pulled at the bed posts and bit into the flesh of her arms. At midnight she lifted herself from the bed and staggered across the floor. It was then the baby was born. The cord had been wrapped twice around its neck.

She lay for hours unconscious beside the dead child.

A drought came. Blair left the place with ninety dollars after a sale.

For fifty dollars he took over the one restaurant in the village. The bulk of the work fell upon Mrs. Blair. There was food to cook and floors to scrub. From the window, when Mrs. Blair had time to look up from her stove, she could see clothes lines, piles of cans and rubbish, and empty liquor crates at the back doors of the five houses on the other street.

Women known as "the girls" lived in the larger house. These girls satisfied the sex desires of men for sixty miles around.

One of these "girls" came the night Leora was born. She told Mrs. Blair that she was a neighbor woman who wanted to help.

It was this woman who brought Leora into the world. She did not leave the house for three days afterward.

Mrs. Blair named her child Leora after the woman. She often talked of the incident. She had not realized that such a girl could be so kind. When Leora was older, her mother told her of the girl whose name she bore.

Leora was not amazed. In all the years to come she was never to pass judgment on another woman.

In spite of the hardship endured in the West, Leora's mother longed through the years for the wide land and the open skies again.

Chapter 3

Leora was at the doctor's office before noon. He greeted her cordially.

"I've come to talk to you," she said.

"Yes, yes, my child," returned the doctor, placing both hands on her rich red-brown hair as though in the act of giving his blessing.

He closed the door of his small private office.

"Now," he said, "let us hear all about it."

"It's nothing much," she said, "My body stings—I'm afraid it won't ever turn white again."

"Dear, dear," he touched her tenderly. "We can fix that all right."

"But I don't want anyone to know I came to you—I want to pay you sometime."

He laughed softly, saying, "All right, Leora, let us see."

He pondered for a moment, then asked, "Which part hurts the most?"

"Every part," was her answer.

He placed her on a small table and left the room for a moment and returned with a large bath towel. Turning the girl on her face, he unbuttoned her dress so that her back was exposed. He rubbed it gently; then allowed his hand to stray over her body. Buttoning her dress, he turned the girl over, and touched her knees. She lay quite still as his hand touched her thighs.

"Does it hurt?" he asked.

She touched his forearm and answered, "No, Doctor."

His hand went further and lingered.

The girl did not move.

Suddenly he leaned over, pressed his hand more firmly against her body, and kissed her fervently.

Then putting her in a sitting position, he said quickly,

"It will be all right in a few days; just have your mother rub you with witch-hazel and alcohol." He thought a moment, "and you might cut a lemon in half, then dip it In glycerine, and rub your body every day for about a week—that will whiten it."

He again put his hands on her hair and held her face to him, "Come at this time tomorrow," he said as she clung to him.

He watched her down the street and returned to his private office.

"She's been a woman two years," he thought. "We've drifted together like two lost clouds."

An impulse tugged at his throat. "Why in hell did I ever get married?" he asked himself, "with new apples growing every year—I'm stuck in an orchard with one."

He nursed the thought of Leora. He had watched her grow up with the feeling that perhaps some day— He shrugged his shoulders.

His wife knocked at the door and said, "Jonas, your lunch is ready."

"Thank you, Mary," was the return, "I'll be there in moment."

He mixed a solution to steady his churning brain. He watched the purple liquid roll into the white, then set it on a table. Taking a small grain, he placed it in a glass of water and watched rivulets of purple arise to the top.

He stood in deep thought for a few seconds and then said, "Oh, well, it's all too damn much for me," and went to join his wife.

"Did you have an interesting morning?" she asked him.

"Oh, so, so," was the reply. "Little Leora Blair came in—a slight ailment—that's about all."

"She's a beautiful little thing," said the wife. "How will she ever end in such a home?"

"God will watch over her," the doctor replied, with slight mocking.

"Jonas, dear—why do you make light of what you don't understand?"

The doctor did not answer for some time. Then, as one would address a child, he said, "That's all right, dear."

Farway's wife was a beautiful, ailing woman. She was the daughter of a prosperous farmer. While attending college in Cincinnati, she had met her husband. She was still under thirty, with yellow hair, sunken white cheeks, and a slight figure. The doctor had no sex desire for her. It had died within a few months after their marriage, five years ago.

A miscarriage had made her anemic and fretful.

The doctor soon had an affair with a nurse. It lasted three years. To his dismay, she had married an osteopath, while other women went in and out of his life.

He would often see the nurse who had married the osteopath. Though her marriage had not broken the intimacy, it had made it more inconvenient. After each affair, he would smile grimly, as he did not respect osteopaths.

He would always say, "Dr. Milligan," the name of the cheated husband, with a slight sneer.

To gain more freedom he encouraged his wife to spend weeks with her parents. His mother-in-law considered him an ideal husband for such thoughtfulness.

He now said, "It must be lovely in the country, Mary. I'm sure your mother would be glad if you paid her a visit."

"Perhaps I will, quite soon," said the wife.

Leora came the next day. The doctor caressed her as before, then touched her firm breasts. The girl received his caresses willingly.

Buttoning her dress, he placed her on his lap. Both were silent. Finally the girl laid her head on his shoulder, then pulled his face toward her and kissed him.

He rose and lifted her in his arms.

She sighed. Her body went limp with yielding. Satisfied with himself, the doctor seated her on the table and said, "Just a few more days, Leora, and your body will be well and white again."

The girl crossed her legs, while the doctor watched.

"Do you love me a little?" he asked.

"A lot," was the answer.

Hearing footsteps in his outer office, the doctor smoothed the girl's hair, kissed her on the forehead, then opened the door and said formally, "Tomorrow at the same time, Miss Blair."

She thanked him and left the office, while the doctor admitted the caller.

That afternoon, while making his calls, the doctor stopped at the Blair home.

"Just passing by," he said to the father. "I wondered how you all were."

Leora greeted him demurely, her hand lingering in his.

"I'm going for a call beyond Locust Grove," he said. "Perhaps you girls would like to come along."

Leora caught his meaning, "Yes, Sally, let's do," she said.

It was late when they returned. Sally thanked the doctor for his kindness, while Leora allowed her hand to linger in his a moment, then said quickly, "Goodnight," and hurried away.

Chapter 4

Two weeks passed. The doctor's wife was with her parents in the country. The housekeeper had gone for the day.

The doctor carried the girl up stairs and placed her on the large bed in the front room. Leora looked about the room, then said, "Not in her bed."

"Beds mean nothing," returned the doctor. His hand was on her body. As always, she became quiet at his touch.

Removing her clothes, he surveyed her nude loveliness.

Her curiosity was stronger than her desire.

An hour later they rose. Her body glowed. She forgot the slight hurt he had caused.

The fulfillment of an often unconscious dream, she went toward him, holding her clothes before her.

Taking her clothes, he placed her on the bed again. He was more patient. She responded slowly with the rhythm of her body. He crushed her to him, exclaiming, "My God, my God."

Several hours passed. He explained to her the mystery of her body and how she might prevent having children.

She returned home late that afternoon and remained silent upon the bed until dusk. The effect of the doctor's caresses would not wear off. She walked again to his office.

At twelve that night she explained to her mother that she had met the doctor accidentally and had gone to a picture show.

It was the first of many days. She became listless and indifferent when not with him.

Her attitude changed in a few months. While she still liked to be with the doctor, her affection for him was not deep. She came to resent Mrs. Farway.

Not wishing trouble in his home, as Mrs. Farway's parents were wealthy, the doctor secured Leora a position with Dr. Otis Haley, as office girl. Now self-supporting, she soon bloomed into a woman. She was sixteen years old.

Dr. Haley was the wealthiest physician in the county.

He had thick lips and a goatee. His ears were small, and his eyes furtive, rheumy, and large. He belonged to all the clubs in his home city, and was a member of the Queen City Club in Cincinnati. A deacon in the Methodist Church, he was an agnostic at heart. His surgical instruments were scattered about his medical library. Once, when Leora came into the library, she overheard him say to a visiting physician, "How can a man believe in all the Christian tommyrot, after seeing what we have seen, Doctor?"

Leora noticed that the visiting physician kept his eyes upon her, and did not answer his host's question.

Dr. Haley's desire for Leora soon became greater than his friendship for Dr. Farway.

Where Dr. Farway had confidently taken the fort, Dr. Haley, being older, laid careful siege.

Unaware that Leora knew of his intentions, he raised her salary twice, and gave her many presents.

At last the doctor won.

She gave herself to him as casually as she would have crossed a quiet street.

Then remembering her aunt's words, "Never let a man think you're easy," she began to cry.

Dr Haley was a leading citizen. He became bewildered. Nothing could soothe her for some moments. "I'm sorry you did that," she said. "Now I can never get married—what will my husband say?"

As Dr. Haley did not know, he placated Leora with fifty dollars.

Later, when Dr. Haley was in slight doubt about his having been the first to seduce her, Leora became angry and cried, saying over and over, "How could you think of such a thing, Doctor?" After much pleading on Dr. Haley's part, Leora explained that she had ridden a bicycle a great deal the year before.

Satisfied with another conquest, Dr. Haley was no longer in doubt.

She was as casual and indifferent about sex relations with Haley as she was with Farway.

Though she remained discreet with both men, her intimacy with each continued. Dr. Farway gave her money, and Dr. Haley gave her a salary of twenty-five dollars each week.

There had never been so much money in her home before. She

gave Sally thirty dollars with which to buy her mother new clothing. When the mother returned with clothes of varying shades, Leora, irritated, returned to the store with her mother and selected more harmonious colors.

She developed greatly during this period. As she earned more than her father, his fear of her became apparent.

She spent more time with her aunt than ever. Dr. Farway once met them in Cincinnati, where a medical convention was being held. As the doctor was busy during the day, she idled many hours with men her aunt knew.

One tried to seduce her. She laughed at him.

"Who are you savin' it for?" he asked.

"For you, when you get a hundred dollars," was the answer.

Leora received the money, and the man another illusion.

When she told her aunt of the experience that strange woman laughed and said, "You're comin' on—I wish I had had as much brains at your age."

When they returned home a week later Leora went at once to Dr. Farway's office.

"I'm bringing you bad news," she said, "I'm that way for a baby."

The doctor was speechless. Then he thought of a plan. "Why don't you go to Dr. Haley," he suggested, "he'll fix you up for fifty—here it is." He handed her the money. "You can tell him some boy did it." She was at first doubtful. He pleaded with her until she promised to explain it to Dr. Haley. "But don't mention my name to him," said Dr. Farway.

"I won't," returned Leora.

Neither did she mention it to Dr. Haley in the way Dr. Farway had suggested.

Instead, she told Dr. Haley that she was "that way for a baby."

Feeling that he was the only man in her life, he gave her medicine that she did not take, and when she became slightly hysterical, he soothed her with money.

When her imaginary danger had passed, both doctors breathed more freely.

Leora and her aunt laughed about the incidents as they strolled through the hickory woods in front of Red Moll's house.

"Men are like children," said Red Moll, "they're fraid of the dark."

Leora watched the evening star appear and made no answer.

Her aunt resumed, "Men are smart not to want children—it's the women who are dumb. They chatter about motherhood, and get old and gray and fat for kids who'll cut their throats in the end." She pulled a piece of hickory bark from a tree. Beneath the bark were two insects fastened together. "You see," she said, "wherever you go it's the same thing. I get so sick of it I could crawl away and die."

"But didn't you ever care—?" asked Leora.

"No—not even when I was your age—it's all so damned messy," replied her aunt.

Leora was silent as she watched the two insects crawl away.

"It's not what I thought it was either," she said at last. "I could go on forever without it."

"It's a good way to get money though—but whatever you do, don't be cheap," advised her aunt. "You'll get more out of men if you're not cheap."

Such talks may have helped to shape Leora's life.

She looked again at the evening star. Her head raised upward gave the lovely contour of her white throat. A slight ripple of wind blew the red-brown hair about her temples. It blew the collar of her silk blouse until the upper part of her breast was exposed.

Her aunt, gazing at her in the dying light of the day, said more quickly than usual, "You're beautiful as the devil, Leora."

"Was the devil beautiful?" Leora asked without blushing.

"They say he was," replied Red Moll. Pulling another piece of bark from the tree, she added, "It's no wonder he went to hell."

Turning again to Leora, she said, "I don't know who you got your good looks from."

"Wasn't mother good-looking?" she asked.

"Yes," was her aunt's reply, "she had good hair and teeth, and her face wasn't bad—but she was not like you—you have everything—I wonder what'll become of you."

"So do I," returned Leora.

"And I wonder what'll become of your mother if she keeps on having babies—she's going to have another, you know."

Leora's voice raised, "Is she—oh dear!"

"Yes," Red Moll mused, "it's too bad—I feel so sorry for her."

Leora returned home late. Her mother was sewing. All the children were in bed.

Mrs. Blair was bent over a dress, her red hand pulling a needle back and forth.

The three top buttons of her calico dress were open. Her faded hair, that had once been tinted with the sun, was now projected in two long straggles, like bent horns from her head.

She looked up wearily and asked, "Is that you, dear?"

"Yes, it's me," replied Leora, entering the room. "Is it true what aunt has told me?" she asked.

Knowing Leora's meaning, the mother bowed over the dress in her hand and said, "Yes."

"This is terrible, Mother, it's a sin."

Her mother made no answer.

Leora looked at a red mark around a figure on a full calendar. It indicated that a menstruation period had been two months passed for the forlorn woman.

Her mother bit the thread at the end of a seam, and laid the dress down, when Leora turned impulsively and exclaimed, "My God, Mother—it's one squalling brat after another."

Her mother made no reply and Leora went on, "You've got to stop some time."

"What can I do?" asked the mother.

"You might shoot him if he ever touches you again—he's just a God-damned animal."

"You mustn't talk that way about your father," said the mother tiredly.

"I'll talk worse when I see him," was Leora's rejoinder.

"Please don't," pleaded her mother, "it ain't his fault—what's a man to do?"

Mrs. Blair bent toward Leora, who stared at her with set face.

"Don't look at me that way, dear—can't you see I need you— I'm the most alone person in the house—I'm so alone I could cry—" She buttoned the top part of her dress—"it's just no use—I can't figure it all out," she moved closer to her daughter. "Now just suppose I didn't want to have you—where would you be, dear?" She began to cry; then said between sobs, "Some day, Leora, when you're married and a baby begins to come, you'll understand." She looked with apprehension at her still stern daughter, "You wouldn't kill it, would you?"

"Yes, I would," was the sharp answer, "it's not murder to kill what's never lived."

"Are you sure, Leora—maybe it's a soul tryin' to get back to the world again."

"Well, it wouldn't come to this house if it had any sense—and you haven't got any right to bring it here either."

The mother took Leora's hand when she had finished speaking.

"Leora," she said slowly, "there's times I don't know you, you're so strange—you're more like the Blairs than my people—the Flemings were never like that—my mother'd of crawled to save a baby."

"And what for—I'd like to know," snapped Leora.

"Because she felt it had as much right in this world as she had—that's why."

A thought came to Leora. Her face brightened, "But, Mother," she said, "It may be you're not that way at all—suppose I talk to Dr. Haley in the morning—he's very kind, and he'll examine you and not charge me anything." She began to soothe her mother.

"All right," returned the worn woman—"maybe you're right—but I'm so tired—won't you come up, Leora dear, and stay with me until I go to sleep?"

"Sure, Mother," was the answer. Leora picked up the kerosene lamp and lighted her mother's steps up stairs.

She sat on her mother's bed for some moments. Hearing her regular breathing, she undressed and lay down beside Sally.

She stared into the darkness for a long time, and then, as was her habit, she went to the window and looked at the silent river. Rain began to fall. She listened to it rattle on the roof until her eyes became heavy.

Again she lay upon the bed.

The noises of the night became vague and far away.

Soon the beautiful and turbulent daughter of William Blair was at rest for the night.

Chapter 5

When Leora came down to breakfast, her brothers and sisters were already jangling their mother's nerves, "Ma, get me this," and "Ma, where are my clean stockings?" and "Ma, can I go to the picture show this afternoon?" The mother, patient as the future, tried to be everywhere at once and help Sally get breakfast for a hungry brood at the same time.

The spick-and-span Leora ignored all the tribe but Sally, who was bent over the stove. "I want to talk to you after breakfast, Sal," she said.

Sally, the indomitable, merely said, "All right, Lee," and went on with her cooking, while two other children rattled the dishes into place on the table.

The heat from the stove flustered Sally. Her red, round face was already perspiring.

"Take it easy, Sal," suggested Leora.

The gas was weak that morning. Breakfast cooked slowly. "Everybody's usin' too much at once," observed Sally.

"Yes," returned her mother, "everybody's hungry at this hour."

"Pa'll be home and breakfast won't be ready," worried Sally.

"That'll be too bad," said Leora, going to the window of the living-room and looking out upon the withered grass of the yard. She could hear men returning from labor at night, dragging their feet along the quiet street that ran in front of the house.

Soon her father turned in at the broken gate. She walked to the kitchen just as he clattered his tin dinner pail on the sink.

"Hello there," said the mother wearily.

In return he asked, "Ain't breakfast ready yit?"

"No," answered Sally, "the gas is awful weak."

"Well gol darn it—you'd have the same story if I got here at noon."

Suddenly Leora stood before him.

"Mother's not feeling well." Her body rigid with anger, she spoke calmly, "And there's going to be no scolding around here."

The father stepped backward. Leora, still in front of him, said, "You know what I mean—I can't keep you from doing a lot of things—but you're going to be quiet now."

The mother stood, her hands on the back of a chair, while Sally, after brushing the hair from her eyes, poured a mixture of mush into a dish.

Blair for a second was in the mood to rebel. And then, beaten by more than his daughter, he went to the living-room until breakfast was announced.

The meal was cold before the mother could eat. For in spite of Sally and Leora offering to help, she insisted on serving the children.

Leora might have been a society girl slumming, so out of place did she seem.

She looked about at her greedy brothers and sisters in the manner of one who hated poverty with every fibre of her being.

It was at such moments that a shrewd observer might have sensed her greatest quality—a prescience as delicate as the whiskers of a cat—that would pay no price for so-called sin, and while she might go through life with lighter baggage than the philosopher, she would still have, in her own way, as much wisdom.

In school she had slipped through her grades without effort. She might have had a harder time without Sally. But then, there was Sally. And if Sally had not been there, Leora would have found a neighbor girl. Though life may have ground her a grisly flour, according to our notions, she was not one to be without bread.

Sally had perhaps a better mind than Leora in school, or, at least as good. She had to make an effort. Leora made none.

She now ate daintily and precisely, and when the breakfast was over, she took Sally into the living-room.

"Mother's that way again," she confided.

"Yes," returned Sally, "I know."

"How did you know?" asked Leora.

"I could feel it," answered Sally.

"But she's not going to have it," said Leora.

"Why, Leora!" said Sally.

"I mean it." Leora looked defiantly at the dingy street.

"But—but—" Sally groped for words, "it's sent here —God's sending it."

"Let Him send it somewhere else—we've got enough." Leora took Sally's arm. "Now I want you, Sally, to tell Mother you just know she caught cold—you can tell her I told you what Aunt told me—and I'll talk to Dr. Haley today—he might do something in a minute to change everything when he examines her, and she'll never know the difference."

While Sally was trying to comprehend, Leora took her other arm, and turned her so they faced each other —"Then Sally—they've just got to sleep alone—if *he*," she said the word with contempt, "wants a woman, let him go to Maggie Queery down the track."

"But Leora," Sally could say no more.

"Now you talk to Mother today—do you hear."

"Yes, Lee—I will." With eyes full of tears, Sally held her beautiful sister in her arms for a moment.

Leora, not responding to the gesture of affection, stepped away, saying, "Now don't forget what I've told you."

"I won't," returned Sally and went to bring Leora's wrap.

Before leaving, Leora went to her mother. Kissing her cheek as a bird would peck it, she said quickly, "Now cheer up, Mother."

Ignoring her father and the other children, she left the house.

Leora always arrived an hour earlier at the doctor's office. It gave her time with the doctor before the office opened.

The doctor was beyond fifty, and he believed that the night was useful for restoring the battery of life.

Before Leora allowed him to caress her she said to the doctor, "I want to ask you one favor."

"What is it?" he asked impatiently.

"My mother thinks she's that way again, and I want you to examine her."

The doctor, old in the ways of bringing and detouring babies, replied,

"Certainly—she's perhaps not that way at all. She probably caught cold."

"That's what I told her," lied Leora, "but she wants to come to you and make sure."

"All right, my dear—tell her to come tomorrow afternoon."

Leora put her arms about the doctor. For several minutes the man of medicine forgot his trade.

Later, the radiant Leora asked, "Doctor—are things a sin when people are not married?"

It was the doctor and not the deacon who answered. As usual with men of science, he asked another question while answering with,

"Is it a sin to be alive?"

"No—I think it's grand," Leora replied.

"That's your answer," said the doctor, as the first caller rang the bell.

Leora's mind was full that day. How different people were. It occurred again and again to her, as she went about her duties.

She had heard Dr. Farway refer to Dr. Haley as a big man. She had wondered at the time what he meant. She still wondered.

Brusque as the wind, he would snap orders to his patients, and scold little children. He never sent bills to the poor. She had often seen him take half the amount offered by a working man. Many times she had heard him say to a poor woman, "What's it worth to you—pay it when you get rich."

Patients who had certain ailments he would send to Dr. Farway. "He's better than I am on such things—but don't tell him I said so—or that I sent you." When one patient had gone, Leora heard the doctor say, "I can't do it all—and Farway is better," he sighed, "and younger."

"But, Doctor," put in Leora, "why can't he cure his own wife?"

"Maybe he doesn't want to," snapped Dr. Haley.

When Leora returned home that evening, her mother was packing her husband's lunch.

"Mother, I've arranged for Dr. Haley to examine you tomorrow."

The tired woman promised to see the doctor.

There was a bustle in the house as she made ready to go. For the first time in weeks she looked in the mirror, and drew back, with her hands before her eyes. She knew what the doctor would say. Mechanically she bade the children good-bye and went to the street-car. The words of Leora kept drumming in her ears. They had not made her bitter, just more tired. Words no longer bothered her. Of late, her runaway son had obsessed her. He might have written to her, she thought, as the wheels of the street-car clicked over the uneven rails.

Leora did not want another baby around the house. It was a squalling brat to her. In spite of all her years with Blair, his taunts about her getting in the family way always stung Leora's mother. No matter what happened, she could not destroy the baby. She recalled her first baby, born dead. The memory of what that child might have been still haunted her in the night. Being gone, it now lived in her fancy. The reality of her living children helped her not at all in imagining what the unformed might have been.

It would soon be three months. In fear she held the secret from the rest of the family and then, in fear, she had told her sister-in-law. She shuddered again at the thought of not having the baby. That would be murder.

She left the car as it stopped, and waited for one returning home.

The children, in the absence of their mother, were playing somewhere else. Except for Piebald, the large black and white cat, the house was deserted. She stared at the picture of a movie actress in tights which Leora had placed near the living-room door. The thumbtack was loose in one corner. She fastened it again. Then her gaze wandered, unseeing, about the room.

The cat walked across the table in the kitchen. She tried to make it get on the floor; then dropped her hand in weariness and stumbled up stairs.

The cat followed her.

She walked in and out of the pine-boarded rooms. A pain gripped her body. She doubled and clenched her teeth, then stumbled forward once again. To stop her teeth from clattering together, she bit her lower lip. Tears dropped out of her eyes. She sat on the bed where Leora and Sally slept; then bit her lower lip again to drive the sobs back in her throat. With her feet still on the floor, she twisted her body and buried her face in Leora's pillow.

The cat jumped on the bed.

Mrs. Blair sat erect and drove the sobs back in her throat.

She stroked the cat's head as it tried to get into her lap.

She then rose and stumbled to the bathroom.

Several of the children returned home an hour later and shouted, "Mother."

There was no answer. Anxious for play, they rushed out of the house again.

Sally returned in a short while, and called, "Mother, are you home?"

The echo of her words returned to her.

She went into the kitchen and saw the havoc caused by the cat.

A sickly yellow fluid dribbled out of the hole in the can of condensed milk. She picked it up, wiped it, then placed it in the cupboard.

After arranging the dishes on the sink, she went up stairs.

Her mother was stretched across the bed, while the cat sniffed at her body. Sally screamed, and threw a shoe at the cat. It scampered down the stairs in a snarl. She rushed to her mother, then into the yard where the other children were playing. "Run and get Dr. Farway!" she shouted, "Mother's ill!"

The children hurried for the doctor, while Sally ran to the house of a neighbor, and breathless, asked, "Please, may I telephone my sister—my mother's very sick."

"You know where it is, Sally." Old Mrs. Ridge pointed her thumb over her shoulder, and remained seated in her chair, a clay pipe gripped in her hand.

Leora turned from the telephone to the doctor. "Mother's ill," she said, "will you take me to her?"

Doctor Farway was already leaning over Mrs. Blair when they arrived. The children stood silent about. Sally was crying.

Dr. Farway looked up as Dr. Haley entered with Leora. He shook his head from side to side and said to Dr. Haley, loud enough for Leora to hear, "Poison."

Leora clutched her mother's dead left hand. Turning, for a slight moment, with wet eyes, she went to Dr. Farway. "Will you do what you can?" she asked, and added the word, "Please."

Dr. Farway patted her shoulder gently, as a father would a hurt child.

As Dr. Haley approached, the younger man said to her, "We will make the necessary arrangements." Dr. Haley nodded assent.

The two men straightened Mrs. Blair's body and put a sheet over it. Motioning Sally to him, Dr. Farway said, "You must keep the cat out of the house."

All went downstairs but Leora.

The children went ahead.

"She's better off," said Dr. Farway.

"Much," replied Dr. Haley.

A sobbing was heard up stairs.

"You had better go and get her," Dr. Haley said to Sally.

Her arms about her, Leora lay by the side of her dead mother. She clung tenaciously when Sally tried to pull her away.

The corpse nearly fell to the floor. Sally called, "Doctor," from the top of the stairs.

Both men came.

Dr. Haley held the body of the dead woman while the younger man took Leora away.

"He killed her, God damn him," she sobbed again and again.

"No, he didn't, child," said Dr. Farway, "it just happened."

"You know better," she sobbed.

Sally looked in amazement at Leora. It was the first time in her life she had ever been hysterical.

"I'll go and make arrangements," said Dr. Haley, "you stay here, Doctor, and do what you can."

"All right, Doctor," returned Farway.

Forlorn as wind-beaten sheep the other children huddled in the kitchen, as Sally entered. "Denny," she said to her young brother—"will you run and tell Aunt that Mother's dead?"

The snub-nosed little boy with the wet red eyes stepped it way from the huddled group and said, "Yes, Sister."

Sobbing again, Leora clung to Dr. Farway.

Heavy steps were heard. "It's your father," said the doctor, pushing her gently away.

"Who the hell cares?" returned Leora, standing more closely to him. "He's got no more strings on me."

The engine wiper came into the house.

"She's gone," said Dr. Farway.

"I, I—" he said no more, and went up stairs. Leora and Farway followed him. He dropped his hat as he stumbled toward the bed.

His tobacco-stained mustache rose and fell. His cheeks were sunken. His body drooped. His bleared eyes focused on the covered body. He became unaware of his daughter and the doctor.

Reaching the bed, he pulled the sheet from his wife, with a spotted, grease-stained hand. Then he screamed, "Nina! Nina! Oh God! Nina! Nina!"

Leora pulled his arm.

The engine wiper paid no attention, but fell on his knees, moaning.

His words became incoherent. The doctor touched his shoulder. "Please, Mr. Blair," he said.

The husband rose, and stood, sagged in the middle. "I guess I better go tell 'em I won't be to work tonight," he looked helplessly about the room.

"You run and telephone them, Leora," suggested the doctor.

The father stepped to her, and, without saying a word, put his grease-stained hand on her heavy brown hair, "Thankee, Leora, thankee."

She went lightly down the stairs, while her father, seeing his hat, stooped to pick it up. Rising, he turned to the doctor and asked, "Whatever made it happen?"

The doctor did not answer.

"We was happy here. I just got a ten-dollar raise."

"Was anything on her mind?" asked the doctor. "Nothin' that I know of," answered the husband.

"Well," said the doctor consolingly, taking his arm, "women at her time of life become sensitive."

"You must be right, Doctor."

Leora returned, followed by the undertaker, the other children, and two neighbor women.

"We had better go down stairs," said Dr. Farway.

The undertaker and the neighbor women remained.

Soon one of the neighbor women came down stairs and took charge of the home.

A boat went down the river. The water from the paddle-wheel still shone in the sinking sun.

"We can do no more now," said the doctor, "You'd better come with me."

"I'm going to order some flowers," she said to Sally. They passed a flower shop, where she ordered several groups of flowers.

When the doctor told the woman to send him the bill, Leora said, "No—it's my mother."

The woman, as if anxious to oblige at such a time, said to the doctor, "I'll send a lovely bunch of lilies-of-the-valley in your name."

"Do, do," said the doctor.

"Let's ride along the river," suggested the girl.

The leaves of the trees had turned to various colors, and stretched, a miles-long carpet, around a bend in the river, behind which the sun had set.

Night came swiftly. The air was soon filled with sparks from fireflies.

"I wonder where the lightning-bugs go in the winter?"

The doctor, roused from reverie, looked at the girl. She had never seemed so beautiful to him. Stopping an impulse to put his arm about her, he said, "They all die, I suppose."

The girl shuddered, "I hate death." She shook her head quickly. Her hair streamed across her face, "I'd be afraid to die."

"Why—," said the doctor, "you're not afraid to go to sleep—and when you do that you wake up to the same old thing. When you die you might wake up to something different."

"I'd rather wake up to the same old thing," returned Leora.

"It's all in the way we're trained," said the doctor. After lighting a cigarette, he resumed, "There are people in the world who laugh at a death and cry at a birth. I was reading about them the other day."

The girl thought for a moment. "Maybe they're right," she said. Her voice became animated, "Tell me—what did my mother get out of life—one kid after another. Her skirts were always lopsided because of babies pulling at them."

"She fulfilled her purpose in the world," said the doctor, "to bring others into it like herself."

"Well—all I can say is—it's a hell of a purpose—she lived and died like a cow."

"Well, that's all right," returned the doctor, "nature's no more interested in her than if she were a cow."

"What's all this claptrap they teach you in church about then?" she asked.

"You called it—just that—it's too easy to believe—don't you think?" He looked at Leora.

"I don't care about it either way, and I seldom give it a thought, except that I don't want to die."

"That's nothing new," returned the doctor, "Nobody wants to die."

"My mother did," said Leora.

Chapter 6

Red Moll had taken charge of the house when Leora returned. Within a few hours it was in complete order. Neighbors brought food for the children. It appeased their grief, and made all silent but Denny, whose tears fell on the cookie he ate.

The old crone, from whose house Sally had telephoned, surveyed the scene, her clay pipe still in a withered hand. To her ancient husband, for fifty-two years a railroad laborer, she said, "Poor soul—she had to die to get her house clean."

Red Moll was now the general for detail around whom the pathetic army of the Blairs found comfort for their loss.

She seemed no more the sister of Blair than Leora seemed his daughter.

Each soldier in the little army of poverty had his task to do. When Denny asked if his runaway brother was coming to the funeral, his aunt leaned over and talked to him quietly.

He asked no more.

When the funeral was over the children did not know which one they missed more—Red Moll—or the woman in the new-made grave.

Sally took charge of the house. Leora returned to work. She would spend but little time at home unless Red Moll was there.

Two weeks had hardly passed when a monument salesman called on her at the doctor's office.

He had, he explained to her, stones of rare materials that would last forever. People hundreds of years in the future would still remember her mother if a stone of proper material were placed over her grave.

She bought a small stone for fifty dollars—five dollars down, and five each month. After it had been placed on the grave, with her mother's name and age chiseled upon it, the entire family went out to see it.

Like millions who had gone before them, who had lived so much in the present, and now at last were dust, not even Leora realized at the moment that in a few generations at most her mother's name would be forgotten in the town.

She was apprised of the fact when she went to her aunt's home. "It's a lot of hocus-pocus—why didn't you put a geranium on her grave and let it go at that?"

And Leora answered, "I wish I had now."

Red Moll was Leora's only real comfort in the town. Like a bird that felt the itch of its wings—she wanted to go elsewhere—anywhere—to join Alice.

When she mentioned leaving to her aunt, she said—"Why don't you—there's nothing here for you but a lot of men who'll never get their houses paid for—Dr. Haley's rich—and so's Farway—but they're hooked up —if you ever come back you may like the place better, or worse—and either way—it don't matter—we all have to live some place—and this is as good as any—for here you've got the river, the woods, and the sky."

Leora remembered.

She made a final decision when Dr. Haley's wife caught him caressing her. Mrs. Haley came to the office the next afternoon while the doctor was making calls.

An immense woman, her vanity was larger than herself.

"You are quite young," she said to Leora, "Perhaps you would like to see the world."

Leora knew what she meant and asked, "On what?"

"Perhaps money—I do not wish to be embarrassed here where I have lived so long—and Dr. Haley is so well known and highly respected." The heavy woman paused. "As you will learn, no doubt, in time, men at a certain age become very silly— You really do not care for him, and he is all I have. I'll give you five hundred dollars if you leave the city."

Leora's heart jumped, but she asked, "Will that cure the doctor?"

Mrs. Haley's pillowy bosom sank in a sigh. "Perhaps not," was the answer, "but I'll see that a much more elderly and homelier woman becomes his office girl." She half smiled. "It's rather difficult for the doctor to give a correct diagnosis with such a pretty girl as yourself around."

Leora remained indifferent. Mrs. Haley became anxious.

"I'd go to the end of the world if I were as beautiful and as young as you," said Mrs. Haley. "What can you possibly find here? If I could change places with you, I'd go tomorrow." Her eyes roved over Leora. "No beautiful girl ever starved—unless she got her heart in a trap, and I've watched you for a long time, Miss Blair."

Leora looked up. Fearing she had said too much, Mrs. Haley laughed. "I am not at all jealous, not at two hundred and thirty pounds." She moved closer to Leora. Her voice became more pleading. "You are a clever girl. Your head is very old, and your heart is older."

Leora stepped gracefully across the room. The older woman's eyes followed. "You know, Miss Blair," she continued, "affection can become a habit after a long married life. I expected the worst when my husband engaged you, but I've always chosen to talk to his women, not to him—*the women understand.*" She stepped heavily to the window out of which Leora was gazing. "I could go to the courts," she said, "and make myself ridiculous, but even the judge would envy the doctor so lovely a girl as yourself."

Leora said nothing. Mrs. Haley, mistaking her silence, asked, "Are you in love with him?"

"Maybe," she lied.

Surprised, the heavy woman finally said, "You can pick up a man like the doctor any day."

"I'm not so sure," returned Leora.

The words alarmed Mrs. Haley.

The girl still gazed calmly out of the window.

Mrs. Haley became more excited and said, "Even if you were in love with him, no good could come of it.

You wouldn't live with him a year if you had him."

"I would be a better judge of that," Leora teased.

"For your mother's sake," the distracted woman said.

"Let's leave her out of it," suggested Leora. "She's through with men for a while."

"Yes, thank God," sighed Mrs. Haley, "I wish I were.

Leora was again silent. As her life was not involved she could be more calm than the older woman, who now began to talk about morals and a woman's duty to society.

After some moments, Leora said, "I don't know what you mean," and then cunningly, "If I were married to Dr. Haley and he saw something in you that he didn't in me—I wouldn't complain—I'd feel that I didn't own him."

Her words hit Mrs. Haley under the heart. She panted for breath.

Mrs. Haley's mind, like her heart, was now in a whirl. She

dropped all feeling of superiority, and held out her hands, saying,

"It is really serious. It will break my heart." She talked on, and more completely revealed her strong anxiety to the instinctive Leora.

Finally Leora said, "I owe four hundred here. I couldn't get far on five hundred."

Mrs. Haley sighed with relief, "I'll make it seven hundred—in cash," she said.

"All right," agreed Leora, "give me the money and I'll leave right now. You can tell the doctor I went home sick, and no one will ever know."

Mrs. Haley had come prepared.

She counted the money while Leora watched her eagerly. When the heavy woman handed it to her, Leora took it indifferently.

"Of course you will keep your word, Miss Blair."

"I'll be as glad to go as you are to get rid of me," was the answer.

Mrs. Haley's manner changed. "I know you'll keep your word. You are not a bad girl—some day you will also marry, and then you will understand."

Leora hardly heard the words. The money crinkled in her hand as she went for her hat and pocketbook.

Returning to where the doctor's wife stood, she placed the money in the purse.

"Don't worry, Mrs. Haley," she said, "I'll be gone in a few days."

The door closed on her last words.

The doctor's wife stared about the office until long after the echo of the girl's footsteps had died away.

She then sank in a chair until the telephone roused her from reverie.

She waddled to the receiver, and answered pleasantly, "Dr. Haley's office."

"Is that you, dear?" asked a man's voice, "This is Dr. Farway."

"This is Mrs. Haley, Doctor."

"Well, well, well—your voice is as youthful as ever," he said, frowning.

"Thank you, Doctor." Mrs. Haley smiled with satisfaction.

"Will you please tell the doctor I called?"

"Certainly, Doctor."

Farway hung up the receiver as though it burned his hand.

"The damned old crow," he said, "how'd she get there —I wonder what the devil's wrong?"

Leora opened her purse and felt the crisp money as she hurried along the street. Her mind raced with her steps.

She would leave the town forever. How glad she was that she had not run away. She thought of the funeral expenses.

"It will spoil him if I pay them," she said to herself, as she thought of her father, "but it will help Sally and the other kids."

The thought came suddenly—she did not have to leave town—she had seven hundred dollars—she might stay and get more—and then—no—she would leave—she was better off—Alice was doing very well.

She wondered what Dr. Haley would think when he returned to the office and found her gone. How would Mrs. Haley explain to him?

Her mind suddenly fertile with schemes, another idea came to her.

She turned in at the undertaker's place of business.

He rubbed the palms of his hands together and opened his solemn face in a fatuous smile, saying, "Can I do something for you?"

"Yes," said Leora. "I collected some of my mother's insurance. If I pay you two hundred dollars in cash will you give me a receipt in full?"

The undertaker wrote the receipt while Leora, waiting, looked about the room which was lined with coffins.

"Do you ever try to figure who'll fill them?" she asked.

"Not so much that," replied the undertaker, "but I often wonder how I'll ever get them paid for."

The girl pondered, "That's right, you do have to buy them, don't you?"

"Yes, indeed, they don't grow on trees," replied the undertaker.

Still elated with so much money, the idea of coffins growing on trees fascinated her.

Her smile made the undertaker forget his dingy business.

"Are you still working for Dr. Haley?" he asked.

"Yes," Leora replied, smiling, "He sent me to get a coffin for Mrs. Haley."

"She needs one," smiled the undertaker, "though I haven't any large enough."

For several blocks the girl thought of coffins growing like apples on a tree.

The trees multiplied, and all contained coffins. Their handles gleamed in the sun as they swayed back and forth.

She could hear the wind swishing around them.

Suddenly one fell to the ground. The lid flew open. Her mother stepped out. Shuddering, she ran a short distance to banish the thought of coffins from her mind.

Chapter 7

Her father was rocking in his chair when she arrived. His wife's death had made him abject.

"I've been thinkin'," he said, a whine in his voice, "how'd Buddy ever hear about his mother."

"Oh," was Leora's answer, "he may be coming back any day."

Her mind still in a furore, she looked restlessly about the house.

She went to the porch just as Dr. Farway entered the gate.

"I telephoned," he explained. "You were not there."

Her quick mind began to work.

"Mrs. Haley became so jealous, I had to leave—as if I'd have anything to do with him—" she said contemptuously. He looked at her in surprise, as she continued, "I'm afraid it's not over yet. She threatened to drag you into it."

The doctor now looked bewildered as Leora went on, "Mrs. Haley screamed as I left, 'I'll shake the whole town with this—Dr. Farway using you, then turning you over to my husband.'"

Dr. Farway pondered, as Leora put in, "Naturally I wouldn't get you mixed up for worlds."

"What are we to do?" he asked.

It was the question Leora wanted.

"I'd leave town if I had the money."

"Where to?"

"Chicago—Alice Tracy is there." She sighed, "But it costs so much to travel."

She had been the most delightful habit in the doctor's life. Faced suddenly with the possibility of her loss, he was confused. And yet, if she remained, and a rumpus were stirred up— Leora cut in upon his thoughts, "She swears she saw us together at the Norfolk in Cincinnati —that she looked at the register, and came right home and found your wife here. I don't care whether I get mixed up in anything or not. It can't hurt me. You're the only one I'm worried about." She then assured him with, "God knows, Dr. Haley couldn't touch me with a ten-foot pole."

"Suppose I took you to Chicago?"

"When?" she asked.

"Whenever you say .... tomorrow night," said the doctor. "I have to go in three weeks anyhow, I may us well make it now. I'll get the tickets and make the reservations. You can get the train at Bellview."

"All right," returned Leora, "but what'll I live on there?"

"We'll fix that up all right," he assured her.

She smiled as he left. Her mind still racing, she went to her aunt's and explained everything.

"Now what do you want to do?" asked her aunt.

"Call Dr. Haley—if *she's* there, *she* won't know your voice."

Red Moll telephoned.

The doctor answered. Leora took the receiver.

"Hello, Doctor—this is me—are you alone?"

"Yes," he answered.

"Well, Mrs. Haley raised the dickens this afternoon—she said she had people watch—I promised to leave for your sake—if she wouldn't make trouble—I'm at my aunt's—can you drive out?"

Dr. Haley came quickly.

Leora explained further, "She said if I left town she'd say nothing and not sue you for divorce and ruin you—I told her I needed money to travel on, and she said she wouldn't give me a cent—so here I am."

If the doctor's heart was not touched, his purse was.

"What would you need?" he asked.

"Oh, I don't know, Doctor, whatever you think—all I know is I don't want to stay around here and make trouble—I don't care about myself—but you've been so good to me—and if she made trouble for you it might make you lose a lot of practice."

The doctor pulled a leather wallet from his pocket. "I have three hundred with me. That should tide you over for a while." He handed her the money.

"Oh, thank you, Doctor, you're so grand."

She promised faithfully to write to him in care of Dr. Farway.

When the doctor drove away, he said to himself, "Caught again—oh, well—it was worth it."

And Leora's aunt said, "Dear me, Leora—you're hair-trigger smart."

"I have to be—look at all those kids—and poor Sally"; then she laughed, "and poor *me*."

On her way home Leora thought of the many things that had happened in the past few years. They bounced like raindrops from her rapidly hardening mind.

Suddenly in her decision to go she regretted leaving Sally. She had never given her a thought before. And now, for a moment, she was overwhelmed at her loss. Sally had waited on her almost since they were babies. She had never scolded and never complained. When Leora had scolded their mother, Sally consoled her.

Reaching home, she explained to Sally that Dr. Farway had loaned her money—"to get me started." She made Sally, who never talked, promise to be more secretive still—"not a word to Aunt, or anybody," she cautioned.

And Sally, who had the faith of her mother, promised over and over again.

Leora took her to the store and bought her many new things. She gave her two hundred dollars. "Spend this on the other kids, but don't tell where you got it." Again Sally promised.

That evening, as the sun glinted the dust across the room in which their mother had died, Sally began to pack Leora's trunk.

Dr. Farway had bought it for her a year before. Leora had pasted the lid with pictures of film actresses in half-nude costumes.

The two girls looked at the pictures.

"None of them can hold a candle to you, Leora," Sally said fervently.

The words pleased Leora. She kissed her placid sister's forehead.

"Will you miss me?" she asked.

Sally, in whose heart was room for nothing but kindness, held her beautiful sister in her arms and replied, "Miss you, dear. It'll be a double graveyard with you and Mother gone."

Leora paused.

"Mother's better off, Sally. I paid her funeral expenses yesterday." She went to her purse and brought Sally the undertaker's receipt. "She has a little stone over her, and you can plant flowers on her grave every year." She looked at the pictures of actresses in her trunk—"She'll have no more babies, and no more meals to cook. She was even lucky in being buried away over in the corner under that big oak." She looked sternly at her sister, "And for God's sake, Sally, don't be a brood mare for any damn man in this town."

"I won't," said Sally. "I won't have time till these kids grow up."

"My God—I never thought of that, Sally."

"I'm happier doing it—the poor little snotty-nosed things. It's not their fault, or father's either."

Leora looked in amazement at Sally. She had never heard her speak so frankly before. Sally surprised Leora again with, "Aunt was right when she said that both dad and mother were like doorbells—if somebody pushed them, they rang—and now the house is full of kids, and Mother's dead, and Dad might as well be."

"But I'll help with the kids, Sally," Leora promised.

"If you do, or don't, it's all right, dear—and if you ever need me, let me know." Sally looked with admiration at the lithe body of her sister, the perfectly chiseled face, the well-rounded breasts, and her hair in brown waves falling.

"We'll make out some way, Leora, just hoe your own row, and, if you get tired, come home. I'll wait on you." Sally, more moved than usual, still looked at Leora. "Even when I was a little bit of a kid, Lee, I tried to protect you. The Lord knows you didn't need it—but you just seemed like a flower and I was always afraid some one'd step on you. I even felt that way about Buddy." Sally stopped— "But he was a good kid too—I wonder where he is?"

"I'd give anything to know," said the lovely Leora—"He was a good kid—remember, Sally, when some one stole our sled, how he hunted all Saturday and Sunday for it—and then Dad licked him because he didn't get home in time to take Mother to the picture show." Leora went to the mirror, while Sally busied herself with the trunk. Suddenly Sally said, and her voice was slightly thicker,

"I just want you to promise one thing, Leora—that you'll write to me once a month—it won't need to be much; you can just say 'hello' and 'good-bye' for all I care—I like you a whole lot, and I always have—and don't want the other kids to ever forget they've got such a nice sister."

Leora turned from the mirror, "I'll promise to write once a month—maybe more—and I won't forget the kids."

Sally put her arms around Leora. "No don't, Leora, please," she said, "it's not their fault they're here. We've got to give them an even chance with every other kid; then maybe they'll get somewhere."

"I don't know," returned Leora. "Aunt says there never was a right Blair and she's one—look at our father."

"Aunt's wrong," said Sally vehemently. "I'm only a kid, but I can prove it out of my school books—we don't know what these kids will be—how can anyone explain how beautiful you are?"

"Mother was a nice-looking girl," said Leora, turning to the mirror, "and Aunt's still good-looking."

"But neither of them ever had your looks." Sally's voice rose, "And, Leora, it will be a lot of fun just watching these kids grow up." She looked about the house as if they were present. "Look at little Denny—don't you think he's cute, Leora, the funny little nose and the square little teeth; look how he runs after you when you start to work—I'll just bet he'll turn out to be a smart man—then we can be so proud." Sally's eyes danced. "Remember when he cried yesterday, and I said, 'Don't cry, Denny, you're a little man now,' and he said, 'Why baby men cry.'" Sally clapped her hands with love.

Leora kissed her sister and said, "Sally, I'd give anything in the world to be the girl you are."

"Why, Leora," exclaimed Sally, "what in the dickens am I? I'm the head cleaner and the dish-washer. I spread the vaseline on the kids when they hurt themselves."

"But you're more than that, Sally, and I've just now thought about it." Leora rubbed her hands over her breasts, then smoothed her hair back. "But let's not talk about it. I'll write to you—and help—because you're square, Sally— Now let's go over to Aunt's; then we can come back and finish packing."

On the way to their aunt's, Leora said, "You can borrow Eddie Wilson's car tonight, can't you, Sally?"

"Yes, dear."

"The train leaves here at nine. I want you to take me to Bellview. I'll get on there," said Leora.

"We can start at eight. It's only twelve miles," returned Sally, "But how about the trunk?"

"I'll wire or write you when to send it. I want to look around first."

The girls found their aunt quite casual. "You'd better wire Alice you'll be there," she advised. "God only knows where that kid'll be— I'll telephone it from here."

The message sent, the aunt returned to the girls, "I suppose you'll miss your father," she bantered.

"Yes,—like the measles," returned Leora. The aunt half smiled.

As the girls left the aunt said, "I'm with you like I'm with Alice, Leora—if you need me, I'm here."

"All right, Aunt," said Leora, "I'll remember."

While returning home, Leora said to Sally, "Don't tell the kids I'm going for good—one funeral's enough in a year."

"All right, but you must write," insisted Sally.

"I will," said Leora.

She bade all a casual good-bye, and chided her father when he tried to caress her.

Both girls were silent on the way to Bellview. Leora passed the spot where she had seen the fireflies with the doctor. Remembrance of it touched her lightly, as a fleck of snow would a pane of glass. A jubilant feeling came over her. "Well, Sally," she said, "I don't know where I'm going, but I'm on my way. Will you wish me luck?"

"You'll get along all right," Sally smiled, as the small car chugged up the hill to the station.

Dr. Farway was reading a newspaper as the car passed.

Sally cried for a moment.

"Please don't, Sally, I'll write—but don't cry."

Caressing her sister, Leora boarded the car, and was taken to Dr. Farway's compartment.

Sally watched the train until it could be seen no more.

In a few moments she dried her eyes, and turned the little car.

When a few miles from the depot, a sudden impulse made her turn the car toward the cemetery.

For a long time she stood at her mother's grave; then returned to the little car, and home.

Chapter 8

WHEN Dr. Farway became amorous, Leora complained of not feeling well. Unable to master his companion, he went to the lounge car and ordered a drink. He mused over the inconsistency of life. He enjoyed Leora more than his wife in every way. She brought him youth and joy. The thought of divorce as a solution did not once enter his mind.

And now, with a growing practice, and a wealthy, ailing wife, he was digging the rut deeper. He smiled with satisfaction at Dr. Haley. He wondered if he might have caressed Leora. Then he recalled what she had said about him. Lulled by vanity, he dismissed the thought.

At first Leora's mind kept pace with the rolling wheels. It became more steady in a few hours. Her life passed before her like a cinema. Being of a nature that could not long cherish hate, the changing scene made her see her father's plight more clearly. Exhausted at last, she closed her eyes.

When the doctor returned to the compartment, she was asleep.

The doctor looked at her for several moments. Losing restraint, he kissed her on the mouth; then put his arms around her.

"Please don't," she pleaded, "I'm not well—and I'm so tired."

"You don't love me any more."

"Yes, I do," said Leora sleepily, "but don't you understand?"

"Yes, I do," replied the doctor, and then added, "I thought you'd be too homesick to sleep."

"Homesick for what?" yawned Leora.

As the train rushed across the Indiana fields in the morning, Dr. Farway said to his companion, "You'll forget who paid your fare to Chicago, won't you?"

"Why?" Leora asked innocently.

The doctor replied, "It may cause trouble if you talk. You see there's a law called the Mann Act. It makes it a penitentiary offense for a man to travel across a state line with a woman not his wife."

Leora opened her eyes wide, as she said, "You pick the strangest things to worry about."

"I know," he said, patting her hand, "I can trust you."

The train stopped at Englewood.

When it started again, a trainman called, "Chicago the next stop."

"I wired Alice Tracy to meet me, dear."

"Why did you do that?" asked the doctor.

Leora smiled, "I knew she'd know the city. Besides, she never talks."

"Well," said the doctor, "what she doesn't know won't hurt her."

When Alice greeted them at the station, Dr. Farway was in a thoughtful mood.

They rode to the Vaner Hotel.

The doctor could not realize the change that had come over Alice. She was fashionably dressed.

"Do you like the city?" he asked her.

"Well," she paused, "I don't like the city as well as I do my work."

"What are you doing?" he asked.

"I'm a cloak model," she answered.

"I'll register alone," said the doctor, looking at Alice, when they reached the hotel lobby. "Do you wish Leora to stay with you?"

"If she likes," returned Alice. "But I wouldn't spoil your fun for anything."

"Oh that's all right," returned the doctor, "you'll want to visit with Leora."

"All right, we'll telephone you this evening," Alice suggested.

"Okeh, if you miss me, try later," he suggested.

"We will," said Leora.

Again in the taxi, Leora smiled at Alice, saying,

"He thinks I might have him arrested for bringing me here." The girls laughed.

"But don't you love him?" asked Alice.

"I did, maybe, for a little while, I don't know," Leora sighed.

"But how you've changed, and you're prettier than ever—now tell me all the news—does my mother look well?"

Leora and Alice talked for several hours.

When Leora saw the doctor that night he asked her what she intended to do.

"Alice intends to get me work as a model," was the reply.

"But you'll need money to get started."

"Yes," agreed Leora, and waited.

He gave her a hundred dollars, saying, "When you write to me I'll send you more."

"I'll write," said Leora.

"Now don't talk about who brought you here," he warned.

"If you mention that once more, I'll never see you again."

There was something in her manner which made him believe.

More confident, he coaxed her to go to his room.

Leora shook her head. "Never again. That's all over. You're the only man, and you'll always be the only man."

"Suppose you get married?"

"That will be different." She hesitated, "But that's not likely. I'll have to get you out of my mind first."

Dr. Jonas Farway was proud of himself.

Chapter 9

Leora was now of medium height, and slender. Her red-brown hair fell in natural waves to her shoulders. Her mouth was slightly full. There was a glow to her skin. At no time did she look more than a school-girl. Her manner was innocent and trusting. She wore, whenever possible, a white linen suit. Simple and graceful, it added to her appearance of innocence. Plain dark green was another favorite color. A plain gold crucifix attached to a thin chain about her throat was her only jewelry.

From her childhood she had the gift of keeping conversation alive. A constant reader of newspapers, she knew all that was current about leading personalities. She had the manner of one who had always lived in the city.

Alice Tracy was a lithe brunette, slightly taller than Leora. More beautiful than her mother, she had Red Moll's passion for wearing red. In contrast to her vivid taste and coloring she wore her hair severely combed back and tied with a wide ribbon. This accentuated her girlish appearance. She seldom wore jewelry. Her movements were as quick and graceful as her mother's.

Alice had many adventures after leaving home. Like all pretty women she had fought different battles in the war of sex. They had ended in victory, defeat, and surrender, according to the opposing side.

She had left the boat at Louisville to join a carnival company that played across Indiana.

Unlike Leora, she was oversexed. From being "man-crazy" at fifteen, she now blended cunning with desire, and was, as a result, much less a feather in emotional storms.

She had early been the plaything of men who came to her mother's house. Seduced soon after puberty without romance, she accepted without concern.

From then on, she was only miserable when not sharing her body with several men.

She found her way to Mother Rosenbloom as naturally as her native Ohio River flowed to the sea.

After four months at Mother Rosenbloom's house, she was placed in an apartment by a manufacturer of tires. Over seventy, apoplectic, and a widower, he had been a caller at Mother Rosenbloom's establishment for many years.

Mother Rosenbloom, under the name of Mrs. Maurice Thorndyke, had direct connection with his home and private office.

She had studied Alice for a month before suggesting her to adorn an apartment for J. Whitlau Everlan.

Mother Rosenbloom assured Alice of the high honor bestowed, and how, with tact, she could line her nest with gold.

"It will be easy to live with Mr. Everlan," she explained. "You will have none of the cares of a wife and none of the physical violence of living with a younger man. If you do not like the touch of so old a man, you must consider that at least it is less heavy and will leave you with fewer bruises. Though I'm a woman, I feel that most women are silly as geese and less important. And the poor things would mate with eagles. All of this comes from reading romantic novels. It's been my observation, Alice dear, in a life that's already too long, that the more a woman is like a man, the greater she is. And you must realize that even though you are young and beautiful now, it will not last forever. If Mr. Everlan makes a good tire he's entitled to his profit. If he treats you well and gives you an allowance of a thousand dollars a month, he is entitled to obedience and respect. If he should find pleasure in the arms of another girl, you must allow the poor man that—for very soon he'll be dead, and then what? If you are clever you will make yourself so agreeable that you can bind him with an invisible chain that's stronger than steel. If he brings you a toy from the ten-cent store you must be thrilled beyond words. I read a great deal when I was younger, and there was a woman in France who was a whore at heart—she slept with everything—but she held Napoleon—and I remember how the poor man went into her room after she was in her grave, and when he came out he'd been crying.

"She flattered him and petted him; she could read him to sleep—I don't know the answer, neither did Napoleon, but the bitch had no fear. Until she was thirty she was the perfect whore. If anyone asks me what it got her, I can ask them right back what sleeping alone got St. Cecilia."

Alice was never to forget the words that followed. "And remember, dear, you cannot be a perfect whore unless a man likes your body. That must come first. And never contradict him either—if you're wise as Solomon, and contradict him, he'll leave you and sleep with a Salvation Army leader. Whenever a man wants intelligence from a woman, he has none himself—

"If you agree with him, you're intelligent—and if you are brighter than he is and let him know it, you're stupid.

"I've been watching men for more years than you've been in the world and the half dozen big ones I've known have been lonely fellows who didn't care any more about anything than I do.

"Nearly everything is poppycock—it's a sin to sleep with different men in this country—in some other country—maybe Ireland, I hope—" she smiled grimly, "it's an honor. And remember, dear, again, that a woman's like a parrot—she's never any bigger than the biggest man she's known."

That Christmas, at Alice's suggestion, Mr. Everlan bought her many volumes concerning Josephine and other lovely ladies now no more.

Being a leading member of different philanthropic and civic organizations, Mr. Everlan made many journeys about the nation.

A long-distance telephone call generally found her at home. If she were out, the maid could immediately tell the operator where she could be found.

Always circumspect, she made every effort to please Mr. Everlan. Though she had lovers when he was out of the city, she nevertheless brought pleasure to him, and satisfaction to Mother Rosenbloom, who had so warmly recommended her to Mr. Everlan.

When Leora became bored after two weeks of looking about the city, Alice took her to Mother Rosenbloom's establishment.

It was in the center of the one-time "restricted district," and had once known a wealthier day. It was still ornate, with stained glass windows, and the mechanical fixtures of fifty years ago. The gilded gas jets were now wired for electricity. It had many large rooms and gables, and a bow window in front.

Mother Rosenbloom owned four houses on the street. These were well painted, as was the house which she occupied with her girls. The paint was peeled from all the other houses on the street. It was otherwise neglected, as though the citizens were concerned with greater problems than the beauty of a neighborhood.

Negro families had moved within a few blocks of Mother Rosenbloom. She did not complain. All creeds and colors were alike to her.

She gave generously to the Catholic creed in which she had been born. Retaining its larger precepts she would go to church once each month with the comment that she wanted to be on the safe side.

If her vices were great, her understanding was greater. So far as she was concerned all people were weak and erring, and it was best to be tolerant of the major sins so long as they paid well.

It used to be said of a girl when she became immoral, "She's on her way to Ryan Street." It was where Mother Rosenbloom still held sway. She had the only establishment left, and she catered to the elite of the city, or rather—men with money.

Alice and Leora approached the house over which Mother Rosenbloom ruled. "Pay no attention to her," said Alice, "she's as sharp as a razor, but you can make more money here than in any other house."

The door opened. They were taken before Mother Rosenbloom.

Chapter 10

She moved swiftly toward them, more in the manner of one skating than walking.

An Irish woman who had married a Jew, Mother Rosenbloom's name was known wherever sex was bartered.

She was between fifty and sixty, and weighed nearly three hundred pounds. Her breasts were as large as pillows. Her earrings, studded with green and red stones, dangled two inches. The diamond rings on the short third and fourth fingers of each hand were encased deep in flesh. It had calloused around them, giving evidence that the rings had not been removed for years.

Her red-painted cheeks were puffed and dimpled. She wore a gold watch at the end of a long chain. It went up and down like a censor as her heavy body moved forward.

Her immense legs were covered with thin silk stockings, through which stray hairs protruded.

An unusually large woman, about six feet tall, there were no curves to her figure. Except for the immense breasts, it might have been a square block. Her head was large and powerful, her hair a faded russet. Below one ear a grayish brindle tuft protruded. Her mouth was wide, and her false teeth, full of gold in front, were even. Her clothing was expensive. Her moods were as changeable as November weather. She could be precise, dynamic, volatile, full of laughter and anger at nearly the same time. Generally her emotions were facile. Then, at times, she was somber, and full of feeling for a moment. Her eyes were walled, and were curved outward like the bottoms of saucers, giving her great round face even more animation than it possessed.

It was said that in her youth she had been a fine singer. This may or may not have been true, as Mother Rosenbloom hardly ever discussed anything that touched her vitally. At times she was capable of a sweeping gusto, and sang with all her young whores around her, while customers, lulled by a voice rare among women, bought liquor with abandon.

She reduced nearly everything to mockery.

Though Leora and Alice were unaware of it, they were approaching a powerful woman who would have dominated any position in which she happened to be born.

While she did not ask her girls in what creed they had been brought up, she was always pleased to meet a prostitute of her own faith. For nearly twenty years she had had one thousand dollars on deposit, drawing interest—"High Masses for the peace of my eternal soul." It was to be turned over to the Church on the day she died.

She wrapped the chain of the watch around her fleshy hands. Then dropping it, while the watch dangled, she pulled at gold-rimmed spectacles attached to a chain above her melon-shaped left breast. Adjusting the glasses on a nose that had once been aquiline, she looked at the girls.

"Hello, Alice dear," she said, with a sharp tone; then, glancing at Leora, she adjusted the glasses again and asked, "Is this the young filly you telephoned about?"

"Yes, Mother," replied Alice.

The heavy woman stepped around Leora as a shrewd buyer would a horse.

She then stepped closer, and her pudgy hand went down the girl's breasts; then moved upward and rubbed her cheeks. She stepped back again and gazed at Leora.

"She'll do, Alice, indeed, indeed." She shook her head as if an old memory stabbed her. "Dear, dear, dear," she sighed, "what pretty hair, a shade of red." She looked at Leora, "Have you evening gowns—you'll need a dozen."

Alice answered, "Yes," for Leora.

"And how are you, Alice? Is he good to you?"

"Yes, Mother, Mr. Everlan is a fine man."

Her tone changed, "You tell me if he isn't. I don't want my girls abused."

"I will, Mother."

The large woman dropped her glasses.

"Her name, Alice."

"Leora Blair."

Mother Rosenbloom studied for a moment, "Pretty —the first name—the last—a trifle harsh—however, that can come later."

She made a move as if to seat herself in a davenport. Alice started to help her.

Mother Rosenbloom shook her head. "No, no, not that—I can never get out of the God-damn thing." She gave the chuckle of a giantess. Leora smiled. Mother Rosenbloom looked from one girl to the other, "Ah, my dears," she said again, "there was a day—but all that's over and done," she chuckled again, "and now I feel as old and dismal as reading the will at midnight—I can lie awake and hear the leaves rattle in the graveyard."

She sat down, then shook her head swiftly, saying, "Heavens—what a thought—and I never think of it until I see youth." She chuckled again. "A drunken rascal was in here last night singing sad songs, and I made him stop—then I made Mary Ellen—you know Mary Ellen—" she said to Alice—"well, I made Mary Ellen sing something gay—and she sang

'Oh for the life of an osteopath,
To play rummy dum diddle
On somebody's middle—'

The watch shook as Mother Rosenbloom chuckled.

Dr. Farway did not like osteopaths. The girls looked at each other.

"Alice, dear, will you press the bell?"

The housekeeper answered. Mother Rosenbloom did not notice her for a moment. Severely dressed in black, with white apron, cuffs and collarette, and grim as the last hour, she stood, her fleshless six-foot body rigid. Had Mother Rosenbloom searched the world, she could not have found a woman who seemed more out of place.

"Matilda," she asked, "will you bring us some coffee and toast?"

The housekeeper bowed, smiled grimly at Alice, glanced casually at Leora, and left the room.

Within a short time they were seated at an improvised table.

"Now, dear," began Mother Rosenbloom, as she looked at Leora, "Alice has no doubt told you considerable about our house. I try to run a respectable place, and only cater to the best people.

"Upon your deportment here, often your future may depend. It is not my policy to keep a girl over two years. If she hasn't feathered her nest with some good man in that time she may as well become a street-walker or join a church. Wealthy men come here from everywhere, and you must treat them with the respect which their position implies. You'll find, of course, that men are all alike—once in the bedroom they will ask you personal questions—where you are from—who took your virginity, and if you don't think that they are the greatest lovers you have known. You must remember, though they come here, they still like innocence—they will keep you awake bragging about the virtue of their daughters. They will try to rescue you from the life of shame which you lead, forgetting indeed that without them you could not lead it—and, as I explained to Alice when she first came here—you must not go to a room with a man unless you are able to make him believe that you've been waiting for him since you were a child. If you cannot respond to his caresses, you must pretend. You must never tell the truth to any man—always color it up with a little romance. If a bricklayer has seduced you, he immediately becomes a millionaire. A successful girl in a house like this always knows how to imply a great deal. You must listen always.... no matter how silly the story—or how many times you have heard it. Give me two beautiful girls and I will always take the good listener—a woman who can't listen is worse off than a rooster who can't crow—as many men come here to be listened to as for anything else. You must laugh at the proper time, and always call me Mother—even if no one is around—then you will not make a slip when men are about."

Mother Rosenbloom sipped her coffee and sputtered, "This damn stuff tastes like rusty water—I'll fire that Nigger." She became calm again.

"And this is for your good as much as mine—" she paused.... "I don't allow men lovers in the house—or pimps, if you'd rather—that is—you can have a lover here every night in the week, so long as you pay me my half of fifty dollars—the charge for the night, and he buys liquor as often as any other man. This, I have found, protects the girl as well as the house. A man likes what he has to pay for. The minute you start shelling out free, he goes elsewhere and pays for it.

"And you must remember that even a hangman or a lawyer feels superior to a girl in a sporting-house; so always be dignified, for they must not feel that you're anybody's dog who'll go hunting. Every man who comes into the place will talk to you as though he would give you the earth—just let them rave, but don't lose your head, for if you cut their throats they would bleed ice water.

"Make the weakest man you know feel that he is a giant. If he touches you a little, just say something like 'Please don't hurt me, dear, you are so strong,' then watch him perk right up."

The shrewd student of sex looked admiringly at Alice and then toward Leora.

"And learn to wear clothes well; though I must say you look very nice today. Men like a clothes mare—even if she's big as a stallion. And never mention anything about your body. Deep in every man's little head is the idea that a woman is still an angel, and would naturally have no natural functions. There are no toilets in Heaven.

"You must never be self-conscious or ashamed of yourself in the presence of men. You have as much right to sell your body as the priest has to sell a Mass." She smiled, her wide gold false teeth showing.

"If men talk to you about only poor girls being in houses like this, say nothing. There's many a rich whore, and if the poor girls get the kings it's because they're better bedfellows, that's all."

She looked from Leora to Alice.

"What can Mr. Everlan buy nicer than Alice—I'd like to know." As neither girl informed her, the immense woman looked at Leora, and resumed, "I wouldn't talk to you so long if I were not so fond of Alice and if you were not so beautiful.

"But keep your head and heart to yourself—for if you don't kick a man, he'll kick you harder. Don't trust any man. They're all after something. Not even a preacher prays on his wedding night. Mr. Everlan would not stay with Alice tomorrow if she got smallpox or a hump on her back. And don't wait for any of the men who come here to lie to you—lie to them first—and always remember to get your money in advance, for not even the President would want to pay when the horse is limber. And of course you must talk some—but not too much—just start the man talking. If he's a lawyer, just say, 'Dear, I'll bet you make a fine presence in court.' That's all—then ask any silly question so long as it lets him talk about himself. If you find he's a doctor, tell him how soothing he must be—

"Talk always as though you have some money, or your people have. Men like the feeling that you are superior—they wouldn't be interested in Cleopatra if she was in a crib on Placer Street and had one leg."

She swung her watch a few times. "And remember, girls, your chief concern is to make men love you, but not have them jealous of you. And no smart girl can afford to be emotional. I've seen women in my house fall in love with men so ugly they'd stop a clock in a morgue. That would have been all right, but the men had no money. And a man should have something to offer a girl.

"Press the bell, Alice, will you, dear?"

The housekeeper removed the table.

"You'll stay here tonight—will you, Alice—he'll be with his

family—and who knows who may come—" Mother Rosenbloom rose slowly. "I think I'll telephone Mr. Skinner," she said, "and tell him we have a virgin in the house."

Her giantess chuckle came again. Alice laughed merrily.

"Now you introduce her to the girls, dear, and pick a last name for her."

"All right, Mother," returned Alice. She took her cousin's arm and led her toward the reception room, which was commonly called "the parlor."

Mother Rosenbloom left the telephone and strolled about the rooms.

She was proud of her house. She loved the thick rugs under her feet, and the touch of the soft brocade drapes.

Though the house was often flamboyant, it was alive, and everywhere gave evidence of the unusual personality that dominated it.

Bowls of beautiful flowers were scattered over the house. A dozen long-stemmed roses were always in a bronze vase on the piano. Mother Rosenbloom had them changed several times a week.

Chapter 11

Four girls, in evening gowns, lounged about the room. All were in their early twenties.

They rose to greet Alice.

"Mary Ellen," she said to the first girl, "this is Leora Blair."

Mary Ellen stepped forward and bowed in a polite boarding-school manner. She had a florid face, bright, wavy red hair, and large brown eyes. She looked as clean as a new cake of soap.

Leora liked Mary Ellen at once. She extended a hand to her. Mary Ellen held it for a moment and said, "Welcome, Leora."

The second girl stepped forward.

"Leora," said Alice, "this is June Le Fear."

June had straight, jet black hair and light blue eyes, a fine sharp nose, and a very small mouth. Her thick pper lip curved slightly. Her teeth were small and even, and her eyes seemed to be getting ready to cry. Her breasts were firm and hard, and she had the manner and movement of a well-brought-up boy.

She looked Leora up and down after the greeting and said to Alice, "She's nice."

The third girl had hair the color of corn silk, and languorous eyes of a greenish cast. Her complexion, very pale, glowed with a delicate pink make-up. Her hands were slender and beautiful. The color, otherwise lacking in her complexion, seemed to have rushed to them. There was about her an air of complete lassitude, as though the touch of men's hands had been too heavy for one so young and frail.

"Leora, this is Doris Mahone," said Alice.

The girls nodded to each other. Before the fourth girl was introduced, Doris had half reclined on a davenport, from where she gazed at Leora.

The fourth girl had a dimple in the center of her chin, and a copper complexion. She wore her hair in two braids, which hung like immense twisted ropes. Her features were those of an idealized Indian girl's. Her lithe body twisted as she walked. "This is Selma," said Alice, as she took her to the davenport near Doris.

Leora was no sooner seated than June was beside her.

"Now listen, girls," and Alice smiled at them, "Mother wants us to give Leora a new name. She says that Blair is too harsh, that no gentleman would like a girl named Blair."

"I think it's nice," June repeated the name, "Leora Blair."

"Sounds like a firecracker," put in Mary Ellen.

"Of course it's not as beautiful as Mary Ellen—that's like a Sunday school teacher's." June looked at Doris, who nodded.

"Why not call her Nellie—let's see—Nellie Narine," suggested Selma.

"I wouldn't have the name Nellie— I knew a girl called that one time and she died of the old ral," said June.

"Well, what did the name have to do with it?" asked Selma.

"Maybe nothing," returned June, "but just the same I wouldn't want to take a chance."

"Then make it Josephine," suggested Doris, adding, "Josephine Le Grand."

"No," Selma shook her head quickly, "that name doesn't fit her character at all."

All the girls laughed. The name was dismissed.

"Why not Doreen Farway?" Alice laughed outright, while Leora smiled.

"That's not so bad," said June, "that's a nice name—I wish I had it."

Mary Ellen did not agree. "It sounds like the wronged girl in a novel," she said.

"Well, just the same, I like it," said June.

"You would, June—you're so romantic," Mary Ellen smiled.

"Why not let's call her Leora," suggested Alice, "and get her a last name. Mother liked 'Leora.'"

"Then why not Leora Le Grand," put in Doris.

"Not with Le Grand and Le Fear in the same house. The men will know they're not real," said June.

"Well, what do they care what we call ourselves so. long as we give them what they want," said Doris.

"Well, just the same, they do," returned June.

"Make it Leora Lavean," said Mary Ellen.

"Too Jewish—it would hurt her chances with some Ku Klux Klanner or something." Selma threw a braid of hair across her shoulder.

"Then give her an Irish name," suggested Selma, "the Irish would never forgive us."

"Mother might like it."

"It's just as well," snapped Mary Ellen, "a name like that would be hard enough to bear, even in Church."

"Call her Rosy Rosenbloom—after Mother," smiled Doris.

"You mean after Mother's dead—and then she'd haunt us." Selma's lithe body moved seductively across the room. "Why not name her Doreen Dewey," she suggested.

"That would be awful," put in Doris, "the house'd be full of sailors, thinkin' she was Admiral Dewey's daughter."

"Well, what of it?" asked Selma.

"Oh nothin'—except they want to pay a girl twenty cents—Mexican money," Doris answered.

"Maybe you'd rather have the officers," Selma smiled.

"Not me," was Doris' quick reply—"they'd want it for nothin'—and think it was a Naval order."

Leora was amused, as Alice put in, "I'd hate to have you girls name my baby."

"Well you'll have a name for it by the time you have one with Mr. Everlan," again Selma smiled.

"Why, Selma—has he disappointed you?"

"Oh no— I just shut my eyes and dreamed of Santa Claus."

Mary Ellen paid no attention to the badinage. "I'll tell you," she clapped her hands, "Call her Leora La Rue—it sounds Frenchy and high-toned."

"Leora La Rue," several of the girls repeated. Satisfying themselves, they asked Leora in unison, "Do you like it?"

"Very much," returned Leora.

"All right then, it's Leora La Rue," said Alice, as she put an arm about Leora.

Chapter 12

THE doorbell rang.

Mr. Skinner was brought into the parlor.

The girls greeted him cordially, while Alice said to the housekeeper, "Mother wants to talk to him."

The grim woman nodded.

Mr. Skinner, a decaying veteran in the army of sex, was stooped and wrinkled. His face was the color of leather, and sharp as an axe. The housekeeper led him away, while the girls smiled.

He was a tradition of laughter in the house. He believed, as Alice explained to Leora, that Mrs. Rosenbloom's mission in life was to find virgins for him. His price was two hundred a virgin... the girl would receive half. Doris and June had each been "ruined" by him. "You'll earn your money," Doris smiled, "it's like trying to sleep with an eel." She gave a slight shudder. "His damned old hands are never still."

"Give him a line, Leora," said June, "make him feel he's hurtin' the hell out of you. He's a rich old thing."

It was a new experience for Leora. She had, for a moment, a slight feeling of repugnance. June seized the opportunity to caress Leora. "It'll be all right ... just pretend he hurts you and sob a little—he's too darned old to do anything more anyhow."

"And don't mention money to him," said Doris, "Mother'll take care of that. Money spoils the romance for him." Doris looked about the room languidly.

The housekeeper came for Leora.

Alice went with her to Mother Rosenbloom.

Mr. Skinner sat, half dozing, in a chair near by.

"He will talk to you here a while," said Alice, "He wants it just to happen—like you met him and couldn't resist him."

The housekeeper delivered Leora to Mrs. Rosenbloom as stiffly as a sheriff would a convicted criminal to the warden of a jail. Without saying a word, she bowed primly and left.

"Now be shy," said Alice, as Mother Rosenbloom put her hand on the professional seducer's shoulder.

"A little lady saw you passing through the room and wanted to meet you, Mr. Skinner."

His rheumy eyes blinked, as he rose and said, "Ah, so, so."

Leora, half bashfully, stepped before him.

The old man's eyes dilated. He caressed her hands.

"We will go and join the girls now, Mr. Skinner, and do be nice to her, for everything is so strange." Mother Rosenbloom stepped heavily away, followed by Alice.

Once in the room, Leora stood bashfully in a far corner.

"Come, my pretty pet," the old man coaxed. Leora did not move.

He advanced cautiously toward her, while she pushed against the wall, her body a-tremble with what Mr. Skinner thought was fear.

"Why, my dear child—you wouldn't think that I would hurt you, would you?" He touched her lightly. She swayed and fell in his arms. In her helpless position, her breast pressed firmly against him. The perfume of her body went to his ancient nostrils, and roused desire in him, and nothing else.

Feeling that it might be too great a strain for Mr. Skinner to drag her to the bed, she rushed blindly toward it, with her hands over her eyes, and apparently sobbing.

As he drew near she said plaintively, "My mother always told me to be careful—and I know you won't—I'm so young."

Her skirt, by design, was above her knees, and revealed silk-clad legs, more perfect in contour than many which greater men than Mr. Skinner had separated.

He touched one of her knees. It shocked her so much that she fell backward on the bed.

The winds of passion howled through Mr. Skinner. He fussed with Leora until nearly exhausted.

Then she got up.

The old man had never met such a girl. Neither had he ever engaged in such a battle. Even had he been a student of genuine acting, he would have been in no condition to appreciate it. Instead he floundered about the room, driven by an urge greater than himself.

At last he coaxed her to sit on the bed again.

"You'll behave if I do," she pleaded.

"Certainly, my precious," he panted, "I wouldn't harm a hair of your head."

"It's not my hair I'm worried about," she said innocently,—"I promised my mother I'd always be a good girl."

"Why you can be a good girl, dear—such ideas are old-fashioned," explained the veteran in the army of sex.

"My mother didn't think so—she told me to always guard my honor—and I promised."

Leora began to cry.

"Now, come dear, come, come, you can trust me." He touched her cautiously.

"I wouldn't have come here, but I knew Alice, and I told her how poor my mother was, and how much she needed a hundred dollars. She told me about Mrs. Rosenbloom running this school for girls, and that I might get work as a maid."

Mr. Skinner shook his head at such innocence.

"Suppose I offered you a hundred dollars."

"Oh, Mother wouldn't let me take it—she'd scold terribly."

He placed the money in her hand while she protested weakly.

She clutched the money while the ruthless Mr. Skinner attempted to despoil her. Sobbing quietly when he rose, she said pleadingly, "Please don't tell Mrs. Rosenbloom what happened—she may not engage me."

Manfully, Mr. Skinner promised. When Leora entered the parlor later with Mr. Skinner, June was at the piano, playing and singing. Her low voice could be heard

> *Oh give me a home where the buffalo roam,*
> *Where the deer and the antelope play—*
> *Where seldom is heard a discouraging word,*
> *And the skies are not cloudy all day*

The girls induced Mr. Skinner to buy a bottle of champagne. They now gathered, with their withered benefactor, around June.

"I love that song," said Mary Ellen, her brown eyes vivid with joy, as she sang with a rich voice,

> *Ofttimes at night, when summers are bright,*
> *By the light of the twinkling stars*
> *I've stood here amazed, and asked as I gazed,*
> *Does their glory exceed that of ours.*

Mary Ellen put her arm around Mr. Skinner, and turned to the girls and said, "Now the chorus, all together."

A deeper, richer voice than Mary Ellen's joined

Oh, give me a home where the buffalo roam, Where the deer and the antelope play—Where seldom is heard a discouraging word, And the skies are not cloudy all day.

The girls turned and applauded Mother Rosenbloom as she finished singing.

Upon her face was joy, and in her eyes were tears. Alice drew Leora aside.

"Was everything all right?" she asked.

"Yes," replied Leora, "everything is in his head." Then she smiled, "but he gave me a hundred dollars."

"Did he tell you he'd come back again?"

"Yes,—tomorrow night."

"Well," said Alice, with advice that was useless, "string him along."

"I will," said Leora.

They moved closer to June, while the other girls were still debating what to sing next.

"Let's have FRANKIE AND JOHNNIE," Selma suggested.

June began,

> *Frankie she sits in her crib house,*
> *Beneath the electric fan,*
> *Telling her little sister,*
> *To beware of the gawdam man*
> *He'll do you wrong, just as sure as you're born.*

Chapter 13

June, like Leora, had been born in poverty.

Her playground had been a junkyard in Cleveland. At nine years of age, she lost a dime near a railroad station. A man saw her crying and gave her a quarter. It gave her an idea. Whenever possible she would pretend she lost money in a public place and cry as if her heart would break. The ruse never failed to work.

Seduced at thirteen, she was in a whorehouse at sixteen. She was now twenty-one; though she claimed to be eighteen.

More forward than Leora, she was not as intuitive. That which Leora sensed without knowing, June had learned through experience. She had to lose the dime before she learned that crying might evoke the pity of man. Upon her first entrance into a sporting-house, she had trusted a man for the night's entertainment. She had seen him often before, and he had spent money freely. When he had gone the next morning, with a promise to return, the landlady asked her for a division of the night's profits—or five dollars.

"He told me he would bring it to me tonight," returned June.

"I can't wait on a man's word… I want my share now."

For several days June expected him. The man never returned. Then the landlady said, "It's worse than payin' for a dead horse. They'll only pay for a thing like that before they get it."

June trusted men no more.

She was fond of Leora, who, at that time, was unaware that one woman could become overfond of another.

There was something whimsical about her that appealed to Leora.

One quiet evening at dusk, before the men began to arrive, the two girls sat in the parlor watching the blaze in the fireplace. She had told Leora of a handsome man she had entertained a half dozen times some months before. She recalled the pleasant hours with longing, and then said, almost to herself, "I wonder what his name was."

She rose suddenly and kissed Leora on the mouth.

Leora was slightly flustered.

"Some day I'm going to get out of all this."

"Then what?" asked the practical Leora.

"I don't know and don't give a damn—I'm damned sick of sellin' my body."

"You don't sell it—you just loan it for a while."

June looked surprised. "That's right, you do get it back, don't you—I never thought of that." She was silent again before saying, "Then why do these damn-fool dames always talk about selling their bodies?"

"They've got to talk about something," replied Leora.

"Anyhow," continued June, "I've been in houses five years, and that's enough—I've been here a year and a half, and Mother doesn't want a girl in the house over two years... the men get tired of them—and I don't blame them either— I don't know why in the hell they like us as long as they do—what the devil are we—sometimes I feel sorry for the poor bastards who come up stairs with me... but what the hell—if I don't hook them, they will me."

"Were you ever in love?" asked Leora.

June rubbed her firm breasts for a moment before answering slowly, "May—be—once—almost."

"Who?" asked Leora.

"A damn fool whose name I never knew." She rested her deep blue eyes on Leora, then said, "Damn him anyhow—what a hard bastard he was." She smiled faintly, "And I thought I was hard." Her voice rose, "Why he was so God-damned hard the iron rattled in his pockets—there wasn't anything between us—not that he knew—the night he left he called a taxi and says to me, 'Listen, Baby, you ain't goin' to see me no more, see—never no more—see... and if anyone ever asks you if you knew me, tell them yes—I'm Jack the Ripper's bodyguard—see—' He was a good-lookin' son-of-a-bitch, and he murdered the king's English something awful—

"When I said to him, 'Why don't you tell me your name, honey'—I can hear him laughin' yet. He put his arm around me and I thought he'd choke me— 'Catch 'em young, lay 'em hard, treat 'em rough, and tell 'em nothin',' he says."

June shook her head, then pushed a wave of black hair from her temple. "Jeeze," she exclaimed, "What a hard son-of-a-bitch he was...

I think he knew he had me, and do you know, he didn't give a good God damn for me—I'd be exhausted when I got through with him. I'd have one thrill after another, and then I'd pretend, and he'd damn near shake me to pieces—till I was limp as a God-damn rag—then he'd laugh at me."

"What did he look like?" asked Leora.

"I'll be damned if I can tell you exactly. His skin was pounded down on his face like a prize-fighter's, and his shoulders were as big as Mother Rosenbloom's bottom—he had a woman tattooed on his breast. You could see her lyin' naked like she was in a woods, his black hair standin' over her . . . there was big dents in his jaws, and once when I hit him in fun with my fist, I damn near cracked my knuckle—when they yelled that his taxi was down front, he slapped a twenty dollar bill on the dresser, and he'd already paid me; then he says —gurgling the last of the liquor on the table

An old mare and an old whore—
Is only good for a few loads more—

"'So get out of the racket, kid—throw hash somewhere and sleep with a section hand.' Katie heard him tell the driver to take him to the Sherman House. I went there this week on my day off and hung around—but I didn't know his name,—damned if I could locate him."

"Maybe you wouldn't like him if you knew him better," said Leora, by way of solace.

"*Know him better*," June sighed. "That first night with him was enough for me. I think I knew then I'd *met the right guy*."

A silence came between the girls. Finally June said petulantly, "Oh—to hell with it—he was some damn roughneck, I suppose."

She talked no more until her mood became lighter.

She then went to the piano and began to play and sing.

Once in a blue moon,
There will come the right one—

The verse of the song finished, June turned to Leora with, "Were you ever in love?"

"Not yet," she answered. "I thought I was once."

The house doctor came the following Monday to examine the girls for venereal disease.

When he finished his task he reported to Mother Rosenbloom

that all were in excellent health but June.

"What is wrong with her?" asked Mother Rosenbloom.

"A rabid case—she had better go to the hospital at once—it may develop. I'll telephone Judge Slattery; he'll arrange," said the doctor.

"All right—do that—I'll talk to him later."

Mother Rosenbloom twisted the gold chain about her hands, and said slowly, "Well, well—poor June."

The doctor lifted his satchel from the chair and made a few steps toward the door. "It's too bad," he ventured; "it's the first case I've ever found in your house."

The immense woman released the chain from about her fingers. Her words came sharply, "I'll take care of it, Doctor—but you might phone Judge Slattery."

She walked slowly to June's room.

"Well, dear, the doctor tells me you've been elected—I've told you so often to examine men carefully."

June turned suddenly, "*Mother, are you joking?*"

"No, dear, if you'll notice—he did not give you a health certificate."

June stood in her negligee, her pink and white body showing. The heavy distributor of sex gazed at her in admiration before saying, "It's a damn shame, dear—but you'd better go to the hospital quietly—or lie in somewhere. I'm having it arranged."

Confused, June looked about the room.

"Who could it have been?" asked Mother Rosenbloom.

June smiled, and answered bitterly, "Only one—and damn his black heart."

"But why take such chances, dear?"

"He told me he was all right and I believed him. He looked like a stallion." June choked a sob and went to Mother Rosenbloom.

The vast woman held the girl's head for a moment against her wide bosom.

"It will be all right, my dear. You must not let it worry you—such things are harder on women when they worry." Her flabby bediamonded hand patted June's shoulder. At last the girl sobbed several times. "Now you'll feel better—get ready for lunch, dear."

"I couldn't think of it, Mother."

"Come, come, the girls will understand." For a fleeting second Mother Rosenbloom's eyes were sad. Then her lips went tight together. She left the girl's room.

June's place was vacant at the table. Mother Rosenbloom looked at the vacant chair. She rang the bell at her plate.

"Take a tray to Miss June's room," she said. The maid bowed and went to the kitchen.

"As you know, girls—June is ill—she is leaving." There was a direful foreboding in her words.

"Yes, we know," said Selma.

The girls gathered in June's room when the meal was finished.

There was forced gaiety in the house for several days after she had gone.

A month passed.

Three of the girls came forward when told there was a man in the house.

He entered as though nothing had happened. Recognizing the girls, he asked, "Where is my little doll?"

Leora, Selma and Mary Ellen stood rigid as soldiers at attention.

"Where do you think she is, you dirty black bastard?" sneered Selma. "Get out of here, you dog." She ran to the hall where a maid was scrubbing the floor. Seizing a bucket of soapy water, she returned quickly to the parlor and dashed it upon him. "It'll clean you up, you diseased rat."

The man who had been June's hero shook himself and hurried to the door. Selma jumped upon him, put her forearm under his chin and jerked his head back. The maid ran from the hallway to the kitchen. The cook came into the parlor with a rolling-pin. Without saying a word she cracked the man across the head. He shook himself furiously. The girls fell every which way; then rushed toward him, scratching his face and pulling his hair.

Before he could fight his way to the door, Mother Rosenbloom had him by the throat. She swung an arm, heavy as the limb of a tree. Her fist hit him under the eye. The diamonds on her fingers tore gashes in his flesh. "Now hurry out of here," she shouted, hitting him again. His eye began to close.

"Get out, get out, get out, you rat-eyed bastard," Mother Rosenbloom commanded. The cook opened the door. The three girls pushed, while Mother Rosenbloom took his arm and threw him violently into the street.

The five women watched, while he scrambled to his feet and ran away.

"We'll show him where his little doll is," Selma laughed hysterically. Leora took Mother's arm. Trembling with anger, the giant woman left the room in silence.

"We should have done this the first time he came," said Mary Ellen.

"How did we know?" asked Leora.

"That's right," said the dark cook, "how was we to know—no woman kin eber tell nothin' 'bout no man, nohow."

Chapter 14

June's place was taken by a girl who soon came to be known as "Crying Marie." Her eyes were brown and liquid and round as silver dollars. Her form was slender, her abandon a temptation. Her mouth, slightly too large, marred the beauty of her face. But even that was forgotten in the glory of her smile. Her hair was jet black. It verged on deep blue under certain strong lights. Knowing this, Marie always managed at some time or another, in the presence of callers, to stand where the light was reflected upon it.

It was Mother Rosenbloom's custom to inspect all the baggage belonging to a new girl. She also examined very closely her negligee, and all other articles of apparel. "A girl must have plenty of silks and satins in her wardrobe," she would often say, "the feel of such things gets more men that way than anything else."

While going through "Crying Marie's" luggage, Mother discovered a small rawhide whip with a mounted silver handle. She shook her head knowingly, but said nothing, "For, after all," she thought, "if a girl wishes to be whipped and divide the money with me, that is her business."

Marie brought several steady callers. Mother Rosenbloom, anxious to learn who might be the wielder of the whip, would scan each caller carefully. Soon a young man called. His manner was feminine. He was elegantly perfumed, and wore heavy blue eye-glasses. After he had been in Marie's room for some moments, Mother Rosenbloom casually walked down the hallway, and stopped outside the girl's door. She heard the swish of the whip, and the slight sobs of the girl. More satisfied than one who discovers a new comet, she walked away.

She had resolved to say nothing to "Crying Marie." At last her curiosity overcame her. She went to Marie's room, and told her what she had heard.

"Yes," the girl admitted frankly, "it's true—it pays well, and I rather enjoy it."

"Of course," said Mother Rosenbloom, "all you get over the house price is your own, providing the guest is satisfied," and then, indifferently, "What does he pay you for such goings-on?"

"Twenty dollars—and he only whips me between my shoulder blades—I pretend to cry, and he doesn't know the difference. You see—I can bring tears any time I want." As Mother Rosenbloom stared, the girl's eyes filled with tears.

As one lost in a grove of miracles, Mother Rosenbloom shook her head. "You say he pays you twenty dollars?"

"Yes," replied Marie.

"Well, I wish more of the damned men had whips instead of the things they have." Still anxious to learn, Mother Rosenbloom asked, "What the devil ever possesses him to do a thing like that?"

Wiping her eyes, Marie answered, "He claims it's the thrill he gets out of shoving me around, and hearing me beg him not to hurt me—I must do it well, for he's been whipping me for three years."

Mother Rosenbloom said nothing for some time. Marie's small silver clock could be heard ticking in the silence. Mother Rosenbloom compared the time of her watch with that of the clock, then sighed, "Oh well—who can ever figure out a God-damned man?"

"Useless to try," said Marie, as she picked up the clock and wound it. Mother Rosenbloom left with the idea of cultivating the young man.

Marie had a sister a year younger than herself. Their father was the drunkard of a Minnesota village. He often drank until he collapsed, and was dragged from gutter or ditch, unconscious. Daily, he would sweep out the saloon, shine the brass, and clean the windows in return for bed and whisky.

Where he came from, no one knew or cared.

One day an undertaker came to the saloon, and, by chance, began to talk to him. He found him a willing listener.

The undertaker offered him work. By degrees he became interested in the work; he drank less. He assisted in embalming bodies, and was never so contented as when around the dead. He also drove one of the carriages in the funeral procession. Wearing a high hat and a frock coat, he would sit erect and proud all the way to the cemetery.

As the undertaker grew older, he turned over the business to Terry, who was really a silent partner. He made it more prosperous.

His wife became intimate with another man.

The girls could hear them quarreling over the intruder; though even then he did not touch liquor and was still successful in business.

After spending hours on a wintry night with her lover, his wife caught a heavy cold. Influenza followed. She was dead within a week.

He became a drunkard again. His business collapsed as well as himself. His children were sent to an orphan asylum.

Marie had been adopted by wealthy people, from whom she ran away. She remained with them long enough to absorb a taste for good living and a desire for exquisite things.

Her hearing was not quite normal. For fear she would not hear a man correctly, and say the wrong thing, her method was to look at the speaker with wide open eyes after he had finished a speech and say with admiring conviction,

"Aren't you wonderful?"

In this way she made many friends among men.

Chapter 15

MANY of Mother Rosenbloom's girls did not want their friends and relatives to know that they were in a house of prostitution, so it was their custom to have letters mailed to the "professor's" house.

The professor was the piano player. It was his duty every night to play the piano and otherwise make the house merry from nine until three.

An ancient German, he had white hair, stooped shoulders, and a sagging lower lip. He wore a frock coat that had turned yellow, and his Byronic collar revealed a long, leathery, wrinkled neck.

The lower lids fell away from rheumy eyes that seldom moved. He lived alone in a small house at the edge of the city. The girls often visited him on their "day off."

A man with no bad habits, he was tolerant with his associates. With his own passions long subsided, he would listen patiently to the woes of the troubled women around him.

With an excellent knowledge of music, he had played the piano and the violin in Mother Rosenbloom's house for sixteen years. Hn that time he had seen many young women come and go—some had married more or less happily, others had died, some had "opened their own places." All had remembered "the professor."

Once, ill for a month, he was deluged with kindness.

He received so many offers of help that Mother Rosenbloom took charge and allowed each girl to contribute twenty-five dollars, while she contributed two hundred. The old man was sent to the country until he had entirely recuperated.

Each evening when he came to work, the girls would gather around him for their mail. Some would scold when they received no letters. His face would take on a hurt look, as though he had been to blame. He always smiled joyfully when he came burdened with mail.

Leora became one of his favorites. He would rub his fingers over her as one would a piece of rare pottery. She was more silent than the other girls. The old man seldom talked. A bond of silence sprang up between them.

Patiently he would teach her the first principles of playing the piano and watch her delicate hands go awkwardly over the keys. She absorbed considerable knowledge of music through him.

The old man admired Beethoven. While Selma and Leora thrummed the piano with him, he talked of his favorite.

"He was like a lion," explained the professor, pushing his hands out to indicate Beethoven's huge head and long hair. "He could make the thunder come, and the lightning—he was the son of a servant—a giant—a giant."

"Well that's all right, I'm not snobbish—what a hell of a bedful he'd make," said Selma.

The professor, aghast, played the piano slowly.

One evening he brought a letter for "Crying Marie." It had been forwarded to several different cities before reaching his house. He watched her read the letter with intense interest.

She answered it immediately and gave it to the professor to mail.

Within a week, while the old man practiced a new tune on his violin, the doorbell rang.

A stylishly dressed young woman stood before him. "Does Miss Mary V— live here?" she asked.

"No, I live alone here—"

"But I had a letter from this address a short time ago."

"Are you sure?" asked the old musician, and then, "Won't you come in?"

She stepped inside, saying, "Thank you," then answered, "yes, I'm quite sure. She is my sister, and I received this letter from her." She showed the old man the letter.

At first he thought his caller a sister of Leora. He parleyed with,—"A girl did have a room here—is she—" and he described Leora.

"No," was the answer. Then came the description of "Crying Marie." "I would like to take her home with me. I'm her sister."

Then the old musician said, "If you'll wait here I'll bring her to you."

"Thank you," smiled the young woman.

She had been adopted by a poor family, and grew up neglected by her more fortunate sister. The man was a laborer, his wife frowsy, and with a half dozen children. The authorities forced the family to allow her to go to school. She would do the house work before leaving each morning.

Her mind was so apt that when she finished school, the young principal interested several families in her welfare. She was sent to Normal School.

An attachment grew between herself and the principal. They exchanged letters weekly, in which little was said of love. Instead, there was a common interest, an intense joy of learning.

When the girl finished Normal School, they were married in secret. The principal was chosen as superintendent of schools in the largest city of his state. He was thirty-four at the time and the newspapers commented editorially on the high honor bestowed upon him. He sent his wife, who was hardly twenty, to college. Upon her graduation as the valedictorian of her class, her marriage to the school superintendent was announced.

"What," asked Mother Rosenbloom, "brings you here in the middle of the afternoon?"

The professor told his story.

Mother Rosenbloom sent for "Crying Marie" and told her the information the professor had given.

"Is it true?" she asked.

"Yes—it's true."

"Well, then, you must go home with her—take your handbags—get a taxi with the professor—then send me a telegram later and I'll ship your trunk to you—it's less wearing to be a whore in good society than here."

The girl hurried to her room. Soon she was in a taxi with the professor, and on the way to her sister.

Mother Rosenbloom went to inspect the room.

"Crying Marie" had taken the whip with her.

Chapter 16

Mother Rosenbloom straightened the curtains, then rang the bell for the housekeeper.

"Have the trunk here taken to the basement," she ordered, "and telephone the girl whose number I gave you yesterday."

When the housekeeper had gone, the heavy woman adjusted a curtain more nearly to her satisfaction, then said half aloud, "Oh well, they come and they go; dear, dear."

Scanning the room again, she started to close the door as Leora passed. Mother Rosenbloom glanced at her quickly and said, "It's you, dear."

She pushed a lock of hair from Leora's forehead before saying, "Well, Marie's gone. I wonder what will happen in this room next?"

Leora stepped inside the room.

Mother Rosenbloom glanced downward, but could not see the floor for her breasts. Her head went slowly from side to side.

"Do anything as you get older, Leora, but never run a house. There's nothing in it but sorrow. One gets used to a girl and away she goes again." She shook her head dolefully. "You were a baby when the first girl went to bed with the first man in this room." She pulled at the watch chain around her neck. "It's a long time ago. It was a two-dollar house then—I was the first to raise it from a dollar on this street, and all the other girls thought I'd go broke." She sighed. "They didn't know men like I did." She shook her head impatiently. "The idea of a woman selling her body for a dollar! It's shameful!"

She wound the watch chain around her fingers. "Why, they're little more than sluts—and they're always in heat."

Mother Rosenbloom's mood was as heavy as her body.

Leora asked, "Mother, where is the first girl who was in this room, do you know?"

Mother smiled forlornly, "Yes," she answered; "I wish I didn't—and I know who the first man was too—and where he is." She loosened the chain about her fingers. "The man was," she stopped, "well, you'll see him, so it doesn't matter—he was Judge Slattery. He's the biggest man in the state—and hard as a wedding tool if he doesn't like you—and a regular baby if he does. We've known each other a long time—came up in sin together, God have mercy on us both."

The radio could be heard down stairs. "Shut that damn thing off," Mother Rosenbloom called. "It'd wake the dead in London."

It stopped suddenly, while Mother Rosenbloom continued, "The damn things are like drunken whores in church—always chattering and saying nothing. If some one sings a good song, some idiot talks about pills right after." Again Mother Rosenbloom wound the chain around her fingers. Leora could hear it scraping against the diamonds on Mother's hand.

"I thought Santa Claus brought you that radio, Mother," said Leora.

"I guess he did—and no one ever yet shot Santa Claus, but I feel like it every time I hear that damned noise box—why I'd sooner have an auctioneer in the house."

It was a full minute before Mother caught her breath.

Leora smiled. Mother looked at the beautiful girl, and smiled back at her, saying, with a sad note in her voice, "What a lovely thing you are, child—you're only fit for the Pope—damn it, that's sacrilege—but," she sighed, "if I were a man I'd rather spend a wedding night with you than go to heaven in the morning."

The gigantic woman's eyes rested upon her. Leora did not know what to say. Finally she asked, "What about the first woman in this room, Mother? You didn't tell me about her."

Mother looked around the room. "There's nothing much to tell, dear child,—Judge Brandon Slattery kept her a long time. He was nice to her, as he always is to everybody—then she ran away with a dago the judge introduced her to. The judge was hurt in his pride—they found her dead in a few months, and the dago was dead beside her. The papers made a lot of it for a day, and then it died down—as Judge Slattery says, 'as dead as yesterday's headline.' No one ever knew who killed them. When they told Judge Slattery he just said, 'Poor girl—that dago got her no place fast.'"

"You don't mean the judge had them killed?"

Mother Rosenbloom twirled her watch and smiled, "No indeed—the judge wouldn't do that—he's always able to pick up three women if he loses one—most any man is—the judge really

Jim Tully

felt very bad about the whole thing— It's just possible that some one did it thinking they were doing the judge a favor—people love him so much they'd kill for him— I've never seen the like of it in all my born days." With a bewildered expression, Mother Rosenbloom took Leora by the arm and left the room.

"You're meeting Judge Brandon Slattery soon," she said to the girl. "He's a very dear friend of mine. He's the only one like him ever born, and they broke the cradle he laid in. He likes to be rich so he can give things away—and he can do more with a fist full of words than another man can with a whole dictionary, and if he ever saw the inside of a college it was when he went to loan a student money. As I often say, he can charm a bird out of a tree—the dogs follow him on the street, and he runs the state—if I didn't believe in God—I'd believe there was something—that made a man like him."

"There's no politician like him in the world—he really likes people, and he likes to do favors—he's sad when people are sad, and he's hungry when they're hungry there's something eating at his heart— but he's always laughing— One time when he was here with a half dozen big men they all got to talking about the people—one man— he as the Lieutenant Governor then—said that they were a lot of cattle and they'd stamp you to death if you didn't watch them—and the judge said, 'Maybe you're right—I often get blue myself—for in my heart I've always wanted to give them my best, and they take my worst—but it's no use to blame them—what chance have they had—it's a wonder to me they're as fine as they are— I heard a line in a play about a moth flying toward a star—it stuck in my mind ever since,—for that's what they are—only they don't get very far till the sun comes up and burns their wings off—and the birds eat them before they reach the ground.' I knew he meant it—he's that way. He could be a millionaire fifty times over if he wanted to be—and I suppose he's worth a million now—no cloud ever threw rain like he throws money. He has his own doctor and dentist take care of all the poor people he sends to them—and he pays them by the year—one time I asked him why he did it and he said he'd had a toothache once when he was a kid and he didn't sleep for a week."

When they reached the door to Leora's room, Mother Rosenbloom paused in her walk.

"He's often told me that a woman in a house like this could keep a secret closer than any man—and he's really the kindest listener in the world— I'm sure he was meant to be a priest." Mother sighed deeply. "But I'm glad he wasn't—for I'd never know him like I do now—and he's the richest thing that's ever come into my life—and to think that a woman left him for a Dago —but, oh hell—women have no sense—look at the men they marry." Mother Rosenbloom opened Leora's door. "Well, dearie," she said, "you'll have to dress for the evening—and it's getting late." Holding her watch in her hand, Mother Rosenbloom went very slowly toward her own quarters. Leora watched her for a moment, and then went into her room.

She sat on the edge of her bed for a long time. Mother Rosenbloom's words about Judge Brandon Slattery still echoed in her brain. She repeated the name—Brandon Slattery.

She had remembered hearing it several years before, when her father, after reading a newspaper, said that grafters like Brandon Slattery would all be put in the penitentiary. "It's men like him what's wrong with our country," she remembered hearing him shout to her mother.

Certain stray things always remained in Leora's mind—especially if they were something unusual about a person. The unusual thing this time was the name—Brandon Slattery.

There may have been perhaps another reason. She would naturally lean toward anyone whom her father wanted to punish.

As on the day she saw the coffins dangling from a tree, she could now see millions of people with the wings of moths. All were valiantly flying towards the sun.

The old days when she attended the shows with her aunt and Alice returned to her.

With a mind too hard for the usual day-dreams, she was now in fancy at the theatre with Judge Slattery.

She smiled grimly in the mirror. Here she was dreaming about a man she had never seen.

A knock came to her door. It was Mary Ellen. "My, aren't you dressed yet—it's about dinner time. The professor's brought the mail."

She handed Leora a letter. It was from Dr. Farway, and enclosed was a certified check for one hundred dollars. He explained that he would send her a check each month, realizing as he did that her salary while learning to be a model would not be a great deal.

He believed all the lies she had written.

Seeing her set expression, Mary Ellen said, "You look like you've heard from the one and only—tell me what he looks like."

"Oh, he's a man," smiled Leora.

"So is mine—he wants me to come back and marry him."

As the girls gathered about Mother Rosenbloom in the parlor, Leora took her aside and said, "Please, Mother—will you do something for me?"

"Yes, Child—what is it?"

"I would like to meet Judge Slattery."

"I'll arrange it. That is why I told you about him."

Leora had never been so pleased before.

There was a soft light in Mother's eyes.

"Why, Mother," she said, "I'm afraid you're in love with him—is it possible that you're having an affair—."

Mother never sighed more deeply, "No, Leora," she at last said, "I'm sorry—I wish it were true—but there's never been but the one man—there's something inside of me that's always kept me from sampling what I sell."

"Why, Mother," and Leora kissed her heavily painted cheek impulsively.

"Yes, dear—it's the truth—but if I had to pick—his name would be Brandon Slattery." She smiled, "He's not a judge—he just looks like one ought to look—so the people call him that."

Chapter 17

THOUGH Mother Rosenbloom conducted an exclusive establishment, she belonged to the old school of madams. She believed in the "parlor system."

A gentleman caller in many exclusive houses saw only the girl he visited. In Mother Rosenbloom's house all the girls not otherwise engaged went to the parlor each time there was a visitor. The caller made his selection from among the girls. It was the custom for the caller to buy liquor before taking the girl "up stairs."

Mother Rosenbloom believed it was bad luck if a man left her house without spending money.

She clung to her old method for the reason that she believed the minds of men varied. The man who wanted a blonde one night might prefer a brunette the next.

Mother Rosenbloom tried to eliminate jealousy among the girls who stayed at her house.

"There is a man in the world for all of us," she used to say, "and naturally a man cannot take all of you to the room at once."

As a consequence there was a friendlier spirit in her house. A girl with a man guest in her room would praise one of the other girls, and, if possible, create desire in his mind. This method was successful in Mother Rosenbloom's house and often the same caller would take a different girl upon each visit.

Mother Rosenbloom's rule was rigid, but never unfair. She commanded obedience and affection at the same time.

To her, love for men was useless. She tried in every manner possible to crush it out of the hearts of her girls. If she did not like men, she liked women even less. Sex was an eternal war to her, covered by smiles and deceits—but a war in which a truce was always dangerous. If the enemy were too kind, he was considered a fool by Mother Rosenbloom.

She was proud of her girls and protected them at all times. "There's no nicer group of ladies anywhere," she would often say to gentlemen who bought liquor. She selected them with care, and only once was she ever completely disappointed.

A mild-mannered girl came to take "Crying Marie's" place in the house. Though Mother Rosenbloom considered her too flamboyantly dressed, she still had confidence in her judgment that the girl would fit well into the establishment.

Within two weeks the girl became so imperious that Mother Rosenbloom decided to reprimand her. She went to the girl's room.

Before she could say a great deal to her, the girl broke into a torrent of abuse. Mother Rosenbloom clutched her watch with perfect poise and waited for the storm to subside.

She had allowed a canary to be placed each day in the girl's room so that the morning sun could shine upon it.

While the girl still raved, Mother Rosenbloom gazed at the chirping yellow bird.

At last, unable to say more, the girl stood gasping, while Mother Rosenbloom still gazed at the canary.

"Sure, I can leave your damned house," the girl screamed; then rushing toward the canary as if it were to blame for the scene, she grabbed it out of its cage and flushed it down the toilet.

Mother Rosenbloom never moved more quickly. She was too late to save the bird. Trembling with rage, she slapped the girl twice. The girl slumped to the floor.

Mother Rosenbloom looked at the empty cage and sighed.

Then, calling the housekeeper, she said, "Miss Revel has decided to leave."

She remained in her rooms all the rest of the day. Late that night Mary Ellen, becoming anxious about her, timidly rang the chimes at her door.

"Come in," Mother Rosenbloom called.

When Mary Ellen stepped into the room she saw that Mother Rosenbloom's eyes were red. She sat, a crumbling mountain of flesh, on the edge of her bed.

"It was nice of you to come to see me, Mary Ellen—do you girls know that damned little whore killed my canary?"

"No, Mother, we didn't. We just knew she left."

"Well, damn her hide," exclaimed Mother, "it's a wonder I didn't kill her—that poor innocent bird to be killed by a crazy whore."

Mother Rosenbloom sobbed, while Mary Ellen consoled her.

Chapter 18

MARY ELLEN came from a long line of farmers. Her great grandfather had taken up a thousand acres from the government more than a hundred years before.

He built a huge brick house on the farm. It had two stories, a great attic, and was surmounted by a cupola of ten windows. The rooms were all large, high ceilinged, and square. There were deep porches on three sides of the house. The lawn occupied about two acres of ground. Across the drive was a grove of several hundred large native oaks, while around the house were many more.

A flagstone walk led from the house to the roadway.

The house was finished all through in black walnut.

Her grandfather and father were born in this house. "It's a place that has lived," Mary Ellen told Leora, "so many people were born and married and died there. I used to lie awake at night and listen to the wind in the trees and imagine it was their ghosts talking to one another."

When Mary Ellen's grandfather was fifty he married a girl of eighteen. She had ten children.

She would become hysterical and throw herself on the ground each time she discovered herself with child. It would require several people to keep her in bed before the baby was born. Five of her children died in infancy.

"I must take after my grandmother," Mary Ellen said to Leora. "There were bees in her bonnet too."

All in the house were fond of Mary Ellen. She was cheerful, generous, and kind by nature.

She would take long walks in the country at every opportunity and would stop to pat the heads of the horses in the meadows and the dogs who ran toward her.

Her mother was a widow with three children when she married Mary Ellen's father.

They made a compact between them. He would provide a home for her children and be a father to them on one stipulation—that she would have a child for him. They married and settled in the large house.

Mary Ellen was born a year later.

Her childhood was happy.

On summer evenings she would go up to the cupola and remain alone. The farm and the ancient oaks, softened by the moonlight, were very beautiful. The child could see the shadows of the leaves on the "carriage house" and the white road stretching by.

The "carriage house," its ancient glory departed, was now the garage. It was always called the "carriage house."

She would often walk down the road on moonlit nights and call; then wait for the echo of her voice to return, while the crickets and the owls, and other revelers of the night, would make weird noises.

In the early morning the child could hear the cooing of doves in the quiet neighborhood.

Her home was a haven for birds. Her father would not allow a gun on the farm. They nested everywhere in the wide trees and at dawn the place was alive with song.

Each spring the scent of apple blossoms would be heavy in the air. There were rows of apple trees behind the house and when the earth became warm they were a mass of pink and white bloom.

It was Mary Ellen's self-appointed task each year to fill the house with apple blossoms.

The wind would howl on winter nights and the snow would scud against the windows and give the child a feeling of security.

Whole weeks would pass in which the trees were weighted with snow. The sun shining upon them made them gleam like myriads of diamonds.

During the winter there were many entertainments at the school-house, and Mary Ellen, who read well aloud, would always be one of the principals.

As the ground was generally covered with snow, the family would go to the school in a bobsled, the runners creaking over the snow-crusted road.

Christmas Eve was gay in the large house. The family would rise in the morning before daybreak and go down stairs together. A loaded Christmas tree stood near the window.

Each year the threshing machine came to her house, accompanied by a dozen men. It would remain about a week. The air would be full of flying chaff as the grain was threshed. The women of the house prepared food for the men.

There was a picture of a farmer wearing a straw hat, a wide smile, and holding a scythe, on the threshing machine. Beneath his picture, on a scroll, was printed, "The Farmer's Friend."

The threshing machine company offered a prize of twenty-five dollars one summer to the boy or girl under fifteen who wrote the best essay on "The Farmer's Friend."

As Mary Ellen was fourteen, she entered the contest and wrote for hours each day, and was awarded the prize.

She was helped in the composition by a young student named Jeremiah Randum.

His father was a large landowner who lived in the County Seat. Jeremiah became attached to Mary Ellen. A studious boy, a few years older than Mary Ellen, he would often tell her how he wanted to become a great lawyer.

She had learned stenography at school and went to work for the summer at the County Seat.

She remained a year, and then secured a position in Chicago.

Jeremiah made her promise to correspond with him. "I'll wait till you're ready to come back," he said, "I'm not the kind that gives up."

She thought of him but seldom in her new world.

In that city she fell in love with a young married man and became his mistress. He deserted her in two years. During this time she corresponded with Jeremiah, who was now a lawyer.

She had a nervous breakdown after the desertion of her lover.

Bitter and cynical, she returned home for a visit.

Her tactful mother talked to her about Jeremiah. She would not listen.

The farm had lost its early glamour.

Jeremiah came to see her as of old.

Saying nothing to her parents about her unfortunate love affair, she returned to Chicago.

A year and a half passed. The melancholy girl met a friend of her ex-lover. With him she went from one dissipation to another, until brought to the attention of Mother Rosenbloom.

That remarkable judge of women knew that Mary Ellen would please her wealthy clientele. She was not mistaken.

Mother Rosenbloom., in Mary Ellen's words, "took the kinks out of her."

In a burst of confidence one evening she told of Jeremiah's loyalty, while Leora and Mother Rosenbloom listened.

"He's been elected district attorney," she said, "the youngest in the state—and here I am—a wreck."

Mother Rosenbloom grunted, "You're not a wreck,—you're just a God-damn fool. I'd go back and marry him if I had to crawl there."

"But look at my past, Mother," exclaimed Mary Ellen.

"Past be damned—you're a better woman for what you've gone through. He's better off with you—and he should be proud to get you. No whore ever lived who wasn't better than a lousy lawyer."

Mother Rosenbloom rose with difficulty.

"Write him in the morning that you're coming," she said.

"All right, Mother," Mary Ellen said, holding the large woman's hand, "you're a peach."

"Never mind that," said Mother, "don't go on being a God-damn fool."

Chapter 19

MOTHER ROSENBLOOM occupied two immense rooms in a quiet part of the house. A skylight had been cut into the roof. She liked to watch the stars from her specially mounted golden oak bed. All about her bedroom walls were autographed pictures of women who had entertained men in her house.

Many bottles of expensive perfume were in a row on the dresser.

No one dared to enter her room without first ringing a chime outside her door.

She slept but a few hours each night, or rather, before dawn. She did not retire until the girls had their all-night guests and the house was in peace. The revelry would often last until after daylight. Mother would always be awake by six o'clock. Her maid would bring her a cup of black coffee mixed with rum. Mother Rosenbloom would sip it slowly. Then the morning papers would be brought to her. She would begin at the first page and read each column carefully. Her acquaintance over the state was quite wide. She knew the histories and ambitions of politicians and thieves, and all other gentry at the top or the bottom of the social scale.

Her tact in handling people was equal to her disdain for them. She had, through her donations to charities, become a secret power in the city. She had preached for years that her house was a necessary evil, and the citizens, always reluctant to quarrel with a generous giver, accepted her dictum.

On the theory that all the store owners cheated her, she sent either the housekeeper or one of the girls to do her shopping. She trusted few people implicitly, and often said that if one believed the worst of humans he would seldom be disappointed. To all who asked favors she was extremely courteous.

To the girls in her house she was often a trifle aloof. Only at rare intervals did she unbend enough to be completely gentle.

Red-headed women were popular with her. "I'd fill my house with them if I could," she would often say. Her most popular ditty was,

> A lean horse for a long race,
> A black hog for a boar
> A cock-eyed man for a son-of-a-bitch
> And a red-headed woman for a whore

She had no feeling for virtue in women. "What the hell's a virgin for?" she would ask. She would sneer at those who thanked her for gifts. If they did not thank her, she would say that people were all alike.

Only during the Christmas holidays did Mother Rosenbloom ever become tipsy. During that week she would fill her vast body like a tank.

Though her tongue at such times was more sharp, her head remained level.

On Christmas Eve Mother Rosenbloom held "open house." All the customers who called were to be entertained at her expense. While the champagne and wine flowed, she surrounded herself with her girls and entertained the men who called. As usual she showed her disrespect for ruined women by singing, to the accompaniment of the old musician at the piano, THE SONG OF SHIME,

> She was poor but she was honest,
> Victim of the squire's whim,
> First 'e 'ad 'er, then 'e left 'er,
> Going to 'ave a child by 'im.
>
> Then the girl went up to London
> For to 'ide her blessed shime,
> There she met another squire,
> And she lost 'er nime agine.
>
> See 'im in the 'Ouse of Commons,
> Makin' laws to put down crime,
> While the womun that 'e ruined,
> Wanders on through mud and shime.
>
> See 'er in 'er 'orse and carriage
> Ridin' daily through the park,

Though she's mide a wealthy marriage,
Yet she 'as a breakin' 'eart.

In their poor but 'umble dwelling,
Where 'er sorrowin' parents live,
Drinkin' shampigne that she sends them,
But they never can forgive.

It's the sime the 'ole world over,
It's the poor wot tikes the blime,
It's the rich wot tikes its pleasures,
Ain't it all a bleedin' shime?

The enormous madam was often touched by simple things.

One day while Leora and Alice were shopping, they sent Mother Rosenbloom a five cent post card. It had the picture of a church, with a small cemetery beside it. A winding road ran beyond, while tiny black specks, represented birds, flew aloft in the pale blue sky.

A toast was printed on the card,

Health and long life to you,
The husband of your choice to you—Land without rent to you
And death in Erin. . . .

They wrote beneath, "We mean this," and signed the card, "Alice and Leora."

Next morning when the mail came she put her glasses on with a stern expression, and glanced casually at the card. She read the lines, then looked at them more closely, put the card down, wiped the fog from her glasses, then picked up the card again and read the words over several times.

She had the card put in an expensive frame and placed it on her dresser. She did not mention ever having received it to either of the girls.

Mother had another verse in a costly frame. She would often gaze at it on the wall for a minute and walk away—

If you can keep your head when all about you
Are losing theirs and blaming it on you,
If you can trust yourself when all men doubt you,
But make allowance for their doubting too;
  If you can wait and not be tired by waiting,

> *Or being lied about, don't deal in lies,*
> *Or being hated, don't give way to hating,*
> *And yet don't look too good, nor talk too wise.*

Mother Rosenbloom had many superstitions. She would never discuss where they came from. Many of them hinted of a rural background. Once, on a visit to the professor's house, she saw one of his pet hens attempting to crow. She left immediately and could not be pacified. She believed that she would die before morning if she remained.

She shook her head in bewilderment and said,

> *A whistling girl and a crowing hen,*
> *Always come to some bad end.*

If she saw two white horses in succession she would make the sign of the cross upon herself. If she met a red-headed man who was cross-eyed, she would take a slug of brandy as quickly as possible afterward. She believed that if one saw a piebald horse and made a wish directly afterward, it would come true. If sparrows hovered around her back door, some person was corning hungry within a day. She swore that her cook could not drive the sparrows away on the day that Doris Mahone came hungry to her door.

If a girl turned her thumbs inward when she folded her hands it meant that her husband would rule her. If outward, she would rule. If a woman's toes turned in, certain parts of her anatomy were large.

If a bird flew in the house, if a rooster crowed in the doorway, if there was a ringing in her ears, or a window accidentally fell—a friend would die that day.

She would allow no one to lie upon the floor in her house ... that meant an early death for the person so careless.

She would cover all mirrors on the death of a friend, believing that if one saw his own reflection in a mirror three times within a day after the death, that he would be the next to go. If it rained on the first Sunday of the month, it would rain every Sunday during the thirty-day period.

If a girl dropped a knife at her table, it meant that a male visitor was coming. As more men came than ever knives were dropped, this superstition was more easily verified. If one dropped a fork, a woman was coming to the house.

If one counted the vehicles in a funeral procession he would be the next to die.

If one wore a dress made on Good Friday she would never live to wear it out.

If a hair from a girl's head curled in her hand, her lover was true to her. If anyone swept under a chair while a girl was sitting on it, she would not be married for two years.

Rain on a wedding day meant calamity for the married couple in the end. Rain at a funeral signified that the dead would rest in peace. If the sun set clear on the second Tuesday in the month it would rain on the last Friday.

Mother Rosenbloom disliked a thin priest, and believed that he would betray the secrets of the confessional to the bishop.

The house doctor, with droll humor, had given her a Gideon Bible as a Christmas present. It had been stolen from a hotel.

It remained always by her bed, under the reading lamp with the vivid red shade.

She had underlined the words of Job with a red lead pencil,

> *My days are swifter than a weaver's shuttle,*
> *and are spent without hope.*

Chapter 20

The house doctor was much larger around than Mother Rosenbloom and many inches shorter. He was so fat that if one pushed a finger into his body the dent would long remain.

He carried his huge paunch before him as though he were balancing a rain barrel. The flesh had crowded his eyes until they resembled a pig's. Even when smooth-shaven, the black bristles still showed in his face. Behind his ears and above his neck were thin remnants of hair. Otherwise he was completely bald. His neck rolled over his collar.

His movements were quick. He puffed constantly.

It was often hinted that he was Mother Rosenbloom's cousin. They were of the same proportions physically, and each walked with the same quick movement despite enormous weight.

He was not a licensed physician. A specialist in venereal disease, his practice was enormous. He knew nothing of ethics. He would overcharge all patients and now and then treat a poor person for nothing.

His pig-like eyes stared from advertisements in the leading daily newspapers. He had an interpreter for all foreigners. All payments were in advance of treatment.

A strict disciplinarian, if one of his employees happened to be a minute late, he was told that he was destroying the morale of his force. He would run a blind advertisement in the newspapers and send cards to all people who answered to call at a specified time. Such interviews gave him a feeling of importance.

He would expound for hours on the blessings of motherhood. It pleased him to be addressed as "Doctor." Accordingly, Mother Rosenbloom and her girls treated him with the utmost deference.

His chief diversion was fondling the girls at Mother Rosenbloom's house.

As his office was closed on Sunday, he would spend the greater portion of that day with them.

He would boast loudly to them of the great doctors he knew. The medical profession had tried for years to drive him from practice, without success.

He had made a life study of venereal diseases. An errand boy for a doctor at fifteen, he remained with him for nine years. During this time he read and observed everything possible on the subject.

Heavy as he was, his acquired knowledge bore him down. Pompous and pretentious, he was brittle as glass and as easily seen through. No impression remained long with him, and his childish moods were as fleeting as shadows on the ground.

He was never so proud as when accompanied to a public place by a beautiful girl. He became fond of Leora, and took her to dinner whenever possible. He would have his secretary telephone restaurants and hotels. The menu would be read; she would take it down in shorthand and copy it later. He would then tell Leora what each place was serving and ask her to make a choice.

One day he told Mother Rosenbloom of an expensive diamond ring being stolen from the finger of a wealthy woman as she lay in her coffin. The old woman said, "The thief was right, a skeleton has no business with a diamond—but I want to be buried with mine."

The doctor was astonished.

"The vanity of ladies," he said.

No farmer loved the sound of rain in drought more than the doctor the sound of words. The many-colored cloud to the poet, the port of home to the world-wandering sailor, meant no more to them than rolling words to the doctor. He would use all his words on Mother. Though heavy as the earth in movement, his tongue was quick. It relieved Mother's alert mind, and brought her solace when her heart was low.

One quiet day, Mother sat in her stiff-backed chair and discussed the sad riddle of all things with the doctor.

She had not forgotten the canary that was flushed to oblivion. Its cage remained near her for weeks, and she would gaze at it long and often.

"How could that split-tail bitch have killed my canary, Doctor—I ask you?" She shook with anger at the thought—"Why God damn her black soul to hell."

"Do not enrage yourself, Mother. All the preponderant stars are in favor of your meeting the glorious bird again."

"Where, for Christ's sake," exclaimed Mother, "in a sewer?"

The doctor's eyes were full of commiseration.

"Mother," he soothed, "you have too much faith for such a thought. For all you know that bird is not in a sewer, but is flying from star to star, a happy threnody of golden song. Where were you before you came here —some place, surely—as you had no beginning and no end. Neither had that bird."

"Oh hell, if I was any place it was some whorehouse in Iowa—but that bird had no immortal soul."

"How do you know, Mother—would you deny to a bird that which you have in full measure? It's as reasonable to suppose that the bird is immortal as anything else. No fluff of golden feathers was ever made to die. And because it went swooping down in its own Niagara is no sign that it has perished."

"But I can't forgive that damned whore," sobbed Mother. "No one but a whore would do such a trick."

"Wrong again, Mother," said the doctor. "She would have done no differently had she been a Methodist bishop's daughter. She might even have eaten the bird. Had she not been a whore she would have been no differently composed. Slightly more inhibited and repressed, perhaps, but in the main, no different. It is wrong, Mother, to call people names—your intelligence is too vast for that. Let the girl remain a whore—even a canary killer. The multifarious restraints of millions of women have not helped society. They have merely made it more hypocritical and docile. For instance, Mother, where are the whores of my boyhood? All are doing very well indeed. The vast majority of them are now happily married club women, and they belong to all the churches and cults. And many of those who are still my friends have lost the color of their girlhood and the direct honesty they had when content to be simple and satisfied whores."

Mother was chuckling.

"And a few of them are lawyers, Mother, and one, much duller than the rest, is a judge." A note of resignation came into his voice, and he added, "no, Mother, it's a mistake to think that only a whore could have sent your canary to a watery grave."

"All right, Doctor, I'll take it back. My little angel may be hopping around up in heaven, but I saw it go down the sewer—and that God-damn bitch of a whore did it."

The doctor sighed and said, "*Oh well.*"

Chapter 21

When another young prostitute was in legal trouble, Selma engaged a lawyer for her. His fee was a hundred dollars. When Selma called at his office to pay the money, the lawyer became amorous. Selma shook her head, saying, "Your price was a hundred dollars and I paid it—mine is ten."

Selma might have been of gypsy or Indian parents. She did not know. Her mother had drifted to a small town on the banks of the Mississippi River when Selma was three years old. She was too busy with other things to talk much of her past to Selma.

She lived in a hovel along the river, the neighbors said for the favors she gave the man who owned it. As she was broken down, her favors were none too desirable. They were at least equal to the hovel in which she lived.

It was of one room. It contained a chair, a bed, and a rusty stove. The outside was plastered with mud to keep the wind away.

No other children would play with Selma. The neighbors again claimed that the mother entertained the men who floated up and down the river. If this were true, her entertainment was free, as all her days were spent in squalor.

Such things made an impression upon Selma.

Other incidents impressed her more—logs floating down the river, guided by a small tugboat, the crew looking out of the window and waving at her as they passed, the far blue sky with its white-dotted clouds, and the wind making waves of the wheat in distant fields.

Her childhood, if lonely, was not painful. It might have been an unconscious training for a bigger destiny, had it not contained too many other elements. She learned to know the river, the riffraff along its banks, and the animal life in the water.

She had marked a turtle which came to the same neighborhood for eight years. One day it grabbed a stick and clung to it. She suddenly discovered a brass ring which some person had put around its neck. In a few more years, as the turtle grew, the ring would choke it to death. She made the turtle a prisoner, and then, with the help of a young hobo along the river, stretched its wrinkled neck and cut the ring.

They then turned the turtle loose. It hurried away as swiftly as possible, and returned later.

She was seduced at thirteen by the young hobo who had helped her with the turtle. Her mother had furnished him a cot, and he slept under the eave of the hovel. During the day he would wander about the banks of the river, and around the town, and return with faded magazines and paper-bound books. He remained in the neighborhood for nearly three years.

He told her that his name was Eddie Ryan.

"That ain't my name," he said, "but it's just as good as any other. People should change their names, anyhow, like they do their clothes—I mean the rich people."

An adept at begging, he would bring food to the house. Having picked up a knowledge of cooking in many jungles, he could prepare it skillfully.

He had a strange assortment of knowledge. He would tell Selma of far-away places, and of life in large cities. Sometimes he would go away for several days at a time and return with money. As lazy as the river, he did his washing once a week, and allowed his clothes to become smooth, and sometimes even to dry on his body.

If she talked of other boys, he was indifferent. Jealousy over a girl was too slight for one who had traveled so far. From having lived in red-light districts upon the charity of its citizens, he knew much about women. He told her many things she was never to forget. Like Selma, the young hobo was solitary, and was content to be alone.

She would spend hours with him in an old canoe. He would tell her about the moon and the stars and how far away they were. Living simply as a dog, he would often talk of riches to Selma. She would listen more attentively than usual.

One night she asked him more about his life, and where he was born.

"I wasn't born no place," he replied. "All my life I've been driftin' around like the clouds. I don't want to be nothin' but a bum—my dad tried to be somethin' else and all he got was what the little boy shot at."

"But suppose," suggested Selma, "you got to be a rich man."

"I'd still be a bum," was the return.

"But tell me about yourself, Eddie—how'd you ever come to this town?"

"On a freight train. The brakie put me off this side of the bridge. I looked up and down the river, and thought it would be a good place to jungle up. I'd been up in Alaska, and I was tired anyhow—then I saw you playin' along the bank, and I began to talk to you, and here I am ever since."

"But don't you ever get homesick?" Selma asked him.

"No more than a bird. It don't pay to get too stuck on people—you've got to leave 'em anyhow when you die; so you might as well begin right away."

Some Negroes across the river sang,

> *I'm goin' to libe anyhow until I die—*
> *I know this kind ob libin' ain't very high.*

The hobo boy and Selma listened until the echo of the words were lost along the river.

"They've got the right dope," said the boy. "They can talk all they want about a rollin' stone gatherin' no moss, but a ramblin' dog always picks up a bone."

The friendship between them was broken as suddenly as it began.

They were picking clams along the river one April morning when Selma said, as if the thought had just struck her, "You know, Eddie, I'm *that way*."

"That way—what?" asked Eddie.

"You know what I mean—*that way*." He still looked bewildered. "I'm goin' to have a baby."

"A baby—what'll you ever do with a baby—you can't eat a baby."

"No, but I'm goin' to have one—and what's more, I want to have one—I've been hoping a long time, but nothing ever happened."

"So you're goin' to have a baby, huh—and you want one—gosh, but women are funny—what do you want all that trouble for?"

"I don't know—I just do—that's all."

The hobo boy frowned.

To placate him, she said, "And we'll call it after you, Eddie."

"All the people'll laugh," said the boy.

"Mother said it was all right with her—she's glad. Nobody ever knows what we do along the river anyhow."

"Well," said the boy, "you're the one that's havin' it, not me—it ain't my funeral."

No more was said about the coming child.

In two days the hobo boy drifted down the river on a raft of logs.

Selma waved at him at the bend in the river beyond her home. For several hundred feet she could still see him waving.

She never saw him again.

The baby was born. She called it Eddie.

That was seven years before. She left home and became a waitress. Consumed with a passion to better the condition of her mother and child, she worked early and late, and often earned as much as two dollars in tips.

A few men gave her money for favors.

Young hoboes often begged food at the restaurant. She never failed to give them a few dimes, besides the food.

The turn of her life came suddenly.

Three older women sat in the kitchen and soaked their feet in vinegar and hot water at the end of a hard day.

Selma was mending a white blouse near by.

Finally a heavy-set waitress said, "If I was as purty as this kid here, I'll be damned if I'd throw hash all day like she does."

Selma looked up as another waitress asked, "What would you do—buy a mint?"

"No sir—I'd hustle, by God—it beats this all to hell—calloused feet, ugly red hands, fallin' of the womb—and I don't know what else."

"You'd git a disease, and then where'd you be?" asked the third woman, as she lifted a soaked foot from the water.

"I'd be all right," was the answer, "I'd a damn sight sooner have a disease than fallin' arches. A dose ain't no worse than a bad cold nowadays."

Within a year Selma was in a dollar house. In another year she was in a five-dollar house.

She spent her earnings on her mother and child.

Besides these two, the dominant things in her life were memories of a turtle that once had a brass ring around its neck and a hobo boy who went down the river on a raft, and never returned.

Chapter 22

Upon Mother Rosenbloom's strict orders, the doors of her establishment were closed at four each morning. Her girls must have rest.

She had the names of more than a hundred young married women on her list. The hours and days upon which their husbands were absent, and their telephone numbers, the length of time which they could spend with a customer—all was typed opposite their names.

Mother Rosenbloom would often say, in checking over the lists of these young women, "Dear, dear, what's marriage coming to?" and shake her head slowly.

Her six assignation houses were located in quiet aristocratic neighborhoods.

As many beautiful young women with devoted husbands needed time to make the necessary arrangements, her "matinees" were often arranged weeks in advance.

It was never proven that Mother Rosenbloom had ever been connected with blackmail.

Mr. Skinner once had an unfortunate experience in an exclusive hotel room. Two men suddenly burst into the room and caught him in a very awkward position. The girl was supposed to be a sixteen-year-old virgin.

He paid fifty thousand dollars to the men whom he presumed to be detectives when they suddenly displayed badges. Later, feeling that he had been framed, he complained to the police. The girl was questioned severely.

In the language of her world, she "stood up" and denied everything. Mr. Skinner had always been a perfect gentleman with her. Being one of "Mother Rosenbloom's girls" her attitude started the rumor that such girls could be trusted.

Mother Rosenbloom was said to have received half of the fifty thousand.

The day after Mr. Skinner complained to the police, a newspaper reporter called upon him.

He knew the story in detail, and he would like to question Mr. Skinner about certain matters which he wanted to write for the syndicate of papers which he represented.

Mr. Skinner had become more experienced in such matters. He had the reporter's claims investigated. To his horror, he discovered that he was the leading feature writer of the city.

The next day another gentleman called upon Mr. Skinner with an offer of "fixing" the reporter. Fifteen thousand dollars were needed. Mr. Skinner paid.

For future protection, Mr. Skinner was sent to Mother Rosenbloom. "This is one woman I can trust," he said. He had nothing further to do with women outside of her house.

The girl later told her lover the entire story. It was repeated a few times about the city. Fortunately for Mother Rosenbloom, the girl and her lover were killed in an automobile accident soon afterward.

Mother Rosenbloom went to the funeral. Two days before, a gigantic bouquet of flowers had preceded her.

Mother Rosenbloom would sit motionless in her favorite chair for many moments. With her hands resting on her immense paunch, which rose and fell several inches with her breathing, she would stare straight before her.

Only once did she ever mention her husband. It was a quick eulogy to Leora. It was followed as quickly with, "And never get married, dear."

If she had emotion at all, it was buried deep in her tremendous body. She was more kind to such girls as Leora, Alice, and Mary Ellen. But a serious expression followed her lightest caress. It was as if she were suddenly warned of an unseen danger.

Many years before she had become interested in a twelve-year-old orphan boy. He was dark and handsome, and was said to have resembled her husband. She engaged a woman to play the role of mother to him. Mother Rosenbloom visited him once a week, and lavished money and affection upon him. When the boy was sixteen, he ran away and was never heard of again. Mother Rosenbloom had given him money the day before.

Weeks, months, and years passed. Finally Mother Rosenbloom put away the gold-mounted miniature of him.

Mother Rosenbloom was more variable than April. When the

man of all work nearly died, she was deeply concerned, and hurried him to the hospital.

He returned in two days.

Mother Rosenbloom looked at him in amazement and exclaimed, "My God, here you are again, and after all the damn trouble you caused me."

A girl came to the house and was given a room. After a month she developed an intense drowsiness from which she could, with difficulty, be aroused. As in the case of the janitor, she was sent to the hospital, where she died. "She'll get her sleep out now," said Mother Rosenbloom, as she paid the hospital and funeral expenses.

Never an ignorant woman, she had no strong convictions. She did not believe in hell; though she clung tenaciously to the hope that all mortals would have a glorious resurrection, where a God would judge them.

She believed in a whole group of gods, on the theory that if operating one house of prostitution was so much trouble, that surely one world was enough for one God.

She was never more contented than when listening to discussions on the mysteries of life and death, and the riddle of the stars.

The easiest way to get her to buy liquor was to start a conversation on a subject which had no earthly solution.

She would lean forward in her chair, her forehead wrinkled in concentration, her eyes intent on the speaker. She would not voice an opinion. If the conversation lagged, she would ask another question.

One of the secrets of her popularity with men may have been that her curiosity made her an intense listener.

She cultivated the young man who whipped "Crying Marie," until he came to her house regularly after the girl had gone. Her amazement always remained unbounded that a man would rather whip a girl than have sex relations with her.

For all the other sexual aberrations she had the utmost tolerance. It permeated the entire house, and no girl was allowed to discuss openly anything that happened in her room.

She set an expensive table. It was laden with choice fruits, wines, and pastries. She was not a heavy eater, and often lectured the girls on the dangers of sweets. The table was always covered with the rarest of linens.

She would sit at one end, and the girls remained standing until she had been seated.

A maid stood at her elbow. If a girl wished another helping, she asked Mother Rosenbloom. She commanded the maid.

Men of finance trusted her judgment. She believed in two commodities—steel and rubber. She invested ten thousand dollars in one of Everlan's ventures. It grew to three hundred thousand. She then sold half her stock and invested the money in United States bonds, saying, "If the country goes, we all go with it."

Many stories were told of her wealth. As nearly as could be computed, it was beyond a million dollars. A confidential secretary came every afternoon.

Her ramifications in sex reached over the city. She had young women on call at any hour of the day or night. It was sufficient for a man to know that a girl came with a recommendation from Mother Rosenbloom. She once sent six girls across the nation as entertainers for a banker and his party.

Though her name was never mentioned by the leading men among more orderly women, she was a power among them.

Taxi drivers worked for her on a percentage basis. If a man spent a hundred dollars in her house, the taxi driver received ten. Mother Rosenbloom's word was never doubted.

Pay day was every Saturday.

Chapter 23

ONE night it was announced that Judge Slattery was in the parlor. When Mother and the girls hurried down stairs, they found him in the kitchen explaining a new way to cook a turkey.

Mother literally dragged him to the parlor. Leora and Doris stood together near the piano. Mother, good as her word, led him to the girls.

Leora was confused, for the first time in her life, before a man.

He touched her shoulder and said, "Lovely girl, Mother—very lovely."

"She's been waiting to meet you."

"That's fine."

He turned to Doris. "And how are you, Doris—it's been how long now?"

"Over a year," was the answer.

He turned to Mother Rosenbloom, saying, "It's all very strange—it was done by a telephone message—otherwise they'd have hunted her for years—and for what?"

The women did not answer. The judge scanned both girls. "But it's lovely to be young, eh, Mother?"

"But, Judge," said Mother Rosenbloom, "you are always young, and your power is greater than your youth —why the very house blooms when you come."

"It should," said the judge, "it takes me so long."

The women laughed merrily, and Leora patted his strong, florid face, and said, "You giant," and cuddled close to him.

The girls were never so charming as when entertaining great men. It was a rule in Mother's house that all men were considered great who spent freely.

They gathered about the judge, and Selma said, pretending to pout, "It's the first time I've ever been jealous, Leora."

The judge held Leora close to him and petted her, saying, "Don't let them tease you, dear; you know a man when you see one."

Leora's heart beat too fast for words.

"How old are you?" the judge asked her.

She started to say, "Sixteen." The words stopped in her throat.

"Never mind," he said, "We'll call you seventeen." He smiled at Mother Rosenbloom—"Where do you get these beauties?"

"They grow like flowers," replied Mother, "and I picked this one for you."

The judge's arm went about Leora. A current went through her body.

She held him closely for a moment.

He moved slightly from her.

"When is her night off?" he asked Mother.

Both looked at Leora.

"I'll send her to you any night you say," said Mother.

"Well let's see," returned the judge, "make it Thursday."

"All right," agreed Mother.

Doris impulsively turned to Leora and exclaimed, "You lucky thing."

Selma joined them as the judge said, "I'd like to have you all if I were younger—even you, Mother."

All laughed. Then Mother said, "You'd have to be a lot younger."

"Mother's a virgin." Judge Slattery smiled. "Indeed I am—the second time in my life." "She's bragging," said Selma.

"Who really is your lover, Mother?" asked Doris.

"Don't you know?" asked Mother. "Why, he comes here, every night when you girls are in bed. He's forty feet high, and he walks so fast he burns the pavement, and makes the breezes blow."

Judge Slattery listened to the banter with an amused smile.

"Does he pay you in advance?" asked Selma.

"A year in advance," answered Mother Rosenbloom. "And do you really love him?" bantered Doris.

"A woman would be insane not to love him," was the answer.

"And insane if she did, eh, Mother?" Judge Slattery moved toward the door. He still held Leora's arm. "Remember, Mother—Thursday night—at my house."

"Yes, she'll come," said Mother.

So happy was Leora that it did not dawn on her that she had not been asked.

"But can't you stay longer, Judge?"

"Not tonight—the governor's in the city."

The room had the silence that follows a cyclone after he had gone.

Leora's knees bent. She half fell on the davenport. "I wish I could go with him some time," Doris said to Mother—"he's been so good to me."

"Maybe he'll take you some time, dear—but it might cause a scandal if the newspapers found out where you came from."

Mother Rosenbloom looked tenderly at Doris.

Leora went to bed that night with a head full of dreams.

She was really not ill, though she explained to Mother that she had a violent headache and would be unable to entertain any men that night.

Mother understood more than Leora realized.

"That's all right, dear," she said, "if any man comes, why don't you close your eyes and think he's Judge Slattery?"

The tears came to Leora's eyes.

"I can't, Mother—really I can't."

"All right, Child, go to bed then."

Leora kissed Mother's hand.

When she had gone, Mother mused a moment. "She's hard hit—the poor little thing."

It was a sleepless night for Leora. If she stared at the ceiling or closed her eyes the same man was always before her. His name lingered in her mind—Brandon Slattery. It made her ashamed. She felt as though she were walking through a woods and someone hid behind a tree and shot arrows at her. She could think of nothing but being possessed by Slattery, to be held in his arms forever. The thought made her body tingle.

In justice to Leora, she had selected an unusual man —more than six feet tall, and lithe as a hound, weighing above two hundred pounds, his wide mouth, protruding jaw, and heavy curly iron-gray hair denoted a man of tremendous force.

She could understand how Farway and Haley became what they were. They had gone to college. From all that Mother said, he had come from nothing.

"He was a beggar boy—and now look at him," she had said to her.

And Alice had asked, "do you think, Mother, that Mr. Everlan is smarter than Judge Slattery?"

"There's nobody smarter than Judge Slattery," was the reply.

And so Leora dreamed.

Chapter 24

DORIS had come to Mother Rosenbloom in an unusual way. She had been at the house for more than a year. She had run away from a reform school two hundred and seventy miles away. It was bitter cold weather when the maid told Mother Rosenbloom that a young girl wished to speak to her.

The mighty woman was in an evil mood. Walking swiftly and heavily she came into the parlor.

The girl stood before her, hands and cheeks bitten raw with the cold.

Timidly she stepped before the empress of sex and said quietly, "Mother Rosenbloom?"

"Yes, I'm Mother Rosenbloom."

"I'm Doris Mahone—my mother went to the convent with you."

Mother Rosenbloom's eyes moved quickly in her immense moon face.

"And what was her name?"

"Bridget Shugrue."

Mother's eyes closed and opened quickly.

"You're Bridget's daughter, really?" she asked. "Yes. Mother died four years ago. I got into trouble after that and was sent to a reform school. I ran away last week—I came right here, and I'm all tired out." The tears welled to the hurt child's eyes. A ray of kindness passed over the face of Mother Rosenbloom. "Goodness, goodness!" she said quickly.

The girl began to sob. Mother Rosenbloom held her against her huge breasts.

"Now, now," she soothed, "don't cry, don't cry—suppose some one sees you. Why, you're Biddy Shugrue's daughter. Dry your eyes, dry your eyes," commanded Mother.

She held the girl from her with both hands. "Sh'h'h—you must never let anyone see you cry—such things are between you and God, and keep all you can from Him."

She seated the girl on the davenport and rang for the maid.

"Will you have a nice warm meal prepared?"

The maid started away. "And bring brandy and warm water with sugar right away," she called.

"Now tell me about your mother—what a dear girl she was—I know she married that drunken vagabond." "Yes," said Doris, "he's dead, too."

"Well, he should be," added Mother grimly. "To cumber the earth with himself was a sin against the Holy Ghost. But to take Biddy and tear her heart out—that's another matter."

The maid came with brandy and water. The imperious woman took the liquid and handed it to Doris, saying, "Here—drink this—swallow it quick."

She literally threw the empty glass to the maid. "Now tell me about yourself," she said to Doris. "I got in trouble twice—my father the first time."

"God damn his soul," snapped Mother.

"The second time with a boy—I couldn't help it—they sent me away—I nearly died there—two years—I hurt myself getting over the wall—but I got to a straw-stack along the Lincoln Highway and dug in. I stayed there till I was so hungry I made up my mind I'd have to take a chance one way or the other—so, long before the sun came up the next morning I walked along the highway, and pretty soon a truck came along with a big canvas top over it.

"I waved at the driver and he stopped and yelled at me, 'Pile on.'

"He didn't ask me any questions, and he must have driven an hour, then he said, 'It's getting too light now—you better get back inside.' There was a lot of old canvas back there and it smelled of beef—but I stretched out and slept.

"When I woke up the truck was standing still. In a few minutes the driver came. He had a bottle of coffee and two sandwiches. 'Here kid,' he said to me, 'you ain't eat yet,' and he put everything on the canvas.

"When he got me here he gave me fifty cents and he said, 'Now beat it—I don't want to know your name nor nothing about you. So if they pick you up it won't be me that turned copper. I'm on.'"

"And you didn't get his name?" asked Mother Rosenbloom.

"No, he just said, 'Over there's the street-car. It'll get you down town,' and before I could say 'Boo' he was gone."

"Well, what did he look like?" asked Mother.

"One of the pictures of a pirate Mother used to read to me about—he had a long black mustache, and his hat was all crumpled and set on his head every which way. Two of his fingers were off, I noticed, and he was big and strong as an ox. There was a white streak clear across his right eye like a knife had cut it and his cheeks were sunk away in like he was suckin' wind."

"My God!" Mother Rosenbloom's head shook in consternation, "and a man like that had a heart like him."

The maid announced that the meal was ready.

Still lost in thought, Mother Rosenbloom nodded.

"Do you know, dear," the giant woman rubbed the diamonds on her left hand with her right thumb, "I'll bet he's some poor devil who served a term in jail."

She led the girl to the dining-room. "You stay right here," she said. "I'll telephone Judge Slattery. He'll fix everything— They'll never look for you in a ten-dollar house."

Chapter 25

DRUNK on champagne, they came to Mother Rosenbloom's, laughing and singing,

> We're wild and woolly and full of fleas—
> We've never been curried below the knees!
> We're little boys in big men's britches—
> Two no-good all-around sons-of-bitches.

Larry Wirt was nearly thirty; Sammy Klein, the younger, about twenty-six. Wirt was the leader of an underworld gang that collected across the nation. There were six in the gang. The tribute amounted to a million dollars a year.

Sammy was his bodyguard. He had large round eyes, and the expression of a bewildered violinist. Though Sammy had the mild manner of a poet, his soft eyes were tiger-quick. His hand was always near an automatic.

Wirt could not speak one word correctly. His mind was coarse as the gutter from which he came. He had been everything, the manager of a pugilist who could not get out of the preliminary class, a pimp for a whore who fell in love with a traveling salesman, a deserter from the navy, and at last a hijacker who became so unerring in thievery that firms smuggling liquor made him a partner, and long afterward lamented that they had not killed him; for he became all-powerful and made them slaves.

A young man of tremendous resourcefulness and cunning, he might have been the greatest detective in the nation had he chosen the side of the law.

Larry was a braggart, with contempt for all things. He would have disputed the right of way with a cyclone. His courage was tigerish, remorseless, his brain lightning in emergencies.

When war was declared in the gang, he and Sammy Klein stood against the other four.

Sammy's earnings were enormous each year merely because Larry liked him. Larry, being a loquacious fellow from the time he was a gutter-snipe, needed a buffer about him. He had met Sammy as a boy. Sammy had taken Larry to his home. He had a twin sister, who was beautiful and more dreamy-looking than her brother. Sammy's father and mother were orthodox Jews. The father had worked humbly as a tailor for nearly thirty years.

Larry liked Sammy's sister. He was not of Sammy's creed. His parents made no obvious objection to their daughter caring for Larry. But though they said nothing, the daughter understood. She remained loyal to Larry, but did not marry him.

How such men as Wirt come to the surface, ruthless as death, and with less pity than a tornado, is a problem for the future. He was a great organizer. His ancestors were all mediocre. None were murderers.

They spent five nights and hundreds of dollars in Mother Rosenbloom's house. Wirt picked Selma, and Sammy chose Leora.

The girls were excellent company. Selma was just the reckless type that appealed to Larry, while Sammy became fond of Leora.

Mother's shrewd eyes read the young men. She made no comment. On the sixth day, Judge Slattery telephoned. "Be careful, Mother," he warned, "they're hot young men."

Mother understood. It was dangerous to be seen too much in the company of "hot young men."

Mother Rosenbloom appreciated Judge Slattery's warning. She decided to ask them not to come to her house until the war was over.

Debating further, she concluded that she would say nothing to the hot young men. "How could I explain where I found out?" she asked herself.

While a sailor, Larry had loitered about Singapore for many weeks. He left with a mania for Chinese cooking.

Larry was what the house doctor called a male nymphomaniac. While Sammy remained close to Leora, his companion sampled every girl in the house. The house doctor tried to explain Larry to Selma and Mary Ellen on the fourth day. Mary Ellen listened attentively. Selma said abruptly, "He's a wild man."

"But it's his glands, Selma," said the house doctor.

"The hell it is," returned Selma, "I know different. I've slept with him and you haven't."

Larry put Mother Rosenbloom's discipline to a severe test. Though four of her girls were infatuated with him, he made his selections to suit his mood. He would explain it by saying, "I'd have you all in the room if I could."

"Go ahead," Mother would laugh, "it's all the same to me."

None of the girls showed the least jealousy. The last night in the house Larry asked Sammy to change girls with him. "I want to please 'em all before I die," he laughed boisterously.

He stayed the night with Leora, and walked about her room and gazed at the different objects. He ran his hand over the lace bedspread. "Nice, eh, Kid," he said, "I can think of worse places to be tonight… You know," he explained, "I didn't pick you at first—you kinda scared me."

He came to a picture of Judge Slattery. "You know him, huh?—He's a guy—I like men who do things with themselves like he did. He's like me—he used to be a newsboy—and he's dead right too—right as a lump of gold."

He looked admiringly at the girl whose reddish-brown hair fell over her shoulders. "How'd you ever happen to be here?" he asked.

Her red lips parted in a slow smile. "I came to meet you," she answered.

"You're a beautiful damn liar," he returned. "We're different—I don't know why—you act to me like you know my number."

A tire exploded in the street. He jumped up quickly and looked about. Leora stood perfectly still.

Laughing, he said, "they might as well kill a fellow as scare him to death."

Leora seated herself at her dressing-table.

"Tell me, Kid, how'd you happen to be here?" "I heard you were coming," she smiled.

He watched her face in the mirror, and motioned to her, saying, "Come over here—you're as cold as the captain's dummy."

"What do you mean?" she asked.

"Didn't you ever hear of the captain's dummy?" "No," replied Leora.

"Well," said Larry, "when I was a sailor in the navy, my Captain fell in love with a little Jap girl in Tokio. He couldn't take her with him on the ship; so he had a statue made of her out of rubber and velvet, and all the stuffin's. He used to sleep with her every night while we were on the cruise. One night, while the Captain was away, playin' golf or somethin', the admiral sneaked into his cabin, and took a rap at the dummy. Well, as sure as I'm tellin' you, in nine days he had a dose." Larry laughed outright.

"I don't think that's so funny," said Leora.

"Neither did the admiral," and Larry laughed louder than before.

When he left the next morning, he said to Leora, "You're some girl, but I was right the first time—we're different—we're not cut out for each other—you get what I mean, don't you? I'm not the guy for you, but I wish I was. Well, so long, Leora, they ain't nobody kin please 'em all. I've tried."

He gave Leora more money than he had given the other girls. "I'm goin' to give you fair warnin', Kid, you're goin' to go for me before you die, an' when you do, I'll walk all over you."

"When I do," smiled Leora, "I'll let you."

"All right, that's a go, Kid—I never wanted anything bad yet that I didn't git." He felt her firm breast and exclaimed, "Hot dog—*God damn*."

It was Wednesday. Leora and Selma had their "day off."

They had a dinner date with Larry and Sammy at a Chinese restaurant.

The girls were ten minutes late.

Larry and Sammy waited for some minutes in the restaurant when Eddie, the waiter, a young man from their own section, came to wait on them.

Through prudence, or wisdom, he had given up the underworld, much to the amusement of his two friends.

"What are you kickin' outta the job now, Eddie?" Larry asked with a smile.

"Oh, about fifty a week and my cakes," answered Eddie.

"My God," exclaimed Larry—"that wouldn't keep a sparrow."

"I know—it ain't much," returned Eddie, "but I feel better—I don't need to run every time I see a cop now, and I can sleep better nights."

Larry smiled again. "Well, that's up to you, Eddie—you always was a funny guy."

"That's all right, Larry," put in Sammy, "everybody has his own life to live—maybe Eddie feels better. If he's not gettin' such big money, he's not takin' such big chances either."

"What do you mean, chances?" asked Larry.

Two men, wearing caps, entered the restaurant. They walked quietly to the end booth, which contained the hot young men. The first man pointed to Larry and Sammy, and then stepped aside quickly. The other stepped forward. Four bullets were fired.

Two went through their hearts. Two pierced their heads.

The murderers disappeared in the excitement. Leora and Selma, just arriving, saw them enter a powerful automobile. They next watched Larry and Sammy being carried from the restaurant.

Next morning their pictures were on the front pages of all the newspapers.

Mother Rosenbloom, glancing at the pictures, said to Leora and Selma, "I was afraid you girls might join those boys yesterday. I heard they were hot."

Leora and Selma looked at each other, but said nothing.

"They were nice boys too," sighed Mother Rosenbloom, "it's too bad."

Chapter 26

THE girls talked all week of Leora's meeting with Judge Slattery. She was the first girl he had ever invited to his home. Ruled by a heavy Chinese servant he called "John Wesley," his house overlooked Lake Michigan at a lonely point near Evanston.

It was now Thursday morning, and Leora's heart sang as she early drew back the curtains.

Selma met her in the hallway and said with mock seriousness, "when you're Mrs. Judge Slattery, Leora, won't you use your influence to have me appointed a janitress in the State House?"

"And have me made official entertainer to the visiting delegates?" said Mary Ellen.

"You would ask for something like that," Doris said, with raised voice. "You wouldn't get rich at that job—a delegate never has any money."

Mother Rosenbloom sent for Leora later in the day. "The judge won't be able to meet you tonight." Leora's heart fell.

"He's coming here with some newspaper men—he told me to hold you out for him."

Again her heart beat fast.

The hours dragged until nine that night, when the maid admitted a fast-talking, half-drunken, little man wearing a shiny blue serge suit much too large for him.

"I'm from the *Bulletin*," he said, "and I'm here to meet Judge Slattery—he's entertaining the press tonight —giving the moulders of public opinion their yearly glance at women flesh."

His hands were ink-stained. The knowledge that he represented what most men fear gave him assurance. Mother Rosenbloom had told the girls to be particularly nice to reporters. Obeying her without reserve, they crowded about the first arrival. For an hour he was a king in a harem.

"This is the life, girls—when I buy out the *Christian Science Monitor* I'm going to have my own whorehouse. An editor ought to make a great madam—everybody that works for him's a whore—but they're pushovers with round heels, and they don't get paid nothing."

The girls laughed gaily.

"We're going to have some fun tonight, girls—believe me—you'll all wonder where you've been all your life before I get through—why the Empress of Zulu sent for me when she couldn't get satisfied in her own country—if I hadn't stayed over there so damned long I'd be an editor now, and not doing police news for a God-damned paper that nobody reads."

He took one drink after another. The girls, their breasts half showing, crowded about the young man in the shiny suit.

Selma put her arm about the reporter.

He looked at the lovely cavern between her breasts. "Oh boy—get me some champagne—we're going to make a night of this—we'll make things stand that's got no feet—I'll show you gals what the Empress of Zulu just adored."

"Was she pretty?" asked Mary Ellen.

"Pretty's not the word," he answered, as Mother Rosenbloom entered— "She was a lalapalooza—skin like copper and bubbies hard as nails. She certainly got to liking me after that first night—I couldn't understand a word she said, but I didn't give a damn. I wasn't there to talk."

He noticed Mother Rosenbloom.

"Ah, Mother—you remember me—I'm James J. Blaidor—the city editor calls me Bladder—but he's a jealous son-of-a-bitch—he hates anyone who can write—"

The maid stood before him with a glass of champagne. He pinched her cheek. "Now all you've got to do is keep my glass full tonight—you stick with me." He looked at her slender and dark young body, and exclaimed, "God, you remind me of the Empress— She told me I was a God-damned fool to take up writing again— over there I had everything—the whole damned ocean belonged to me—the ships and the sky were mine—and the little gal who waited on the Empress wasn't so bad—they called her the princess of the bedchamber—and the Empress said to me— 'Now treat her nice, J.J.—it's a very small woman who can't share a good thing with another— Coming of a royal line as I do, I'm convinced that the chief pleasure in the world lingers around the womb of a woman'— The Empress was of the opinion that the only enjoyment in life was when you forget—and I used to make her forget—she'd trill like a lark when she forgot— Now don't overwork me, girls— I'm the last stallion in the meadow—when I mount 'em they stay mounted— I'm the Ambassador of Love to the queens of the world—no new method goes into effect at the Hague without my sanction— My grandfather was a great favorite with Queen Victoria

"Where's that champagne?"

The copper-colored maid stood smiling at his side. "Oh, there you are, Empress." He rushed for the glass and began to sing,

> When I was a king in Timbuctoo,
> I made no laws for the very few—
> The rich and the poor
> And the living and the dead—
> Could all have pleasure in their bed.

He held the empty glass out to the maid, saying, "Here, Empress."

Revealing her even teeth in a broad smile, she poured the bubbling liquid into the glass.

"You should live in Zulu, girls," he said, "there's a man for every mood—and they're all rich—

> The people that's in Zulu nor richer nor the Jews—
> There's not the smallest young gossoon but travels in his shoes—

The professor played the tune on the piano, while Doris sang.

The reporter stumbled to a davenport. "I'm all in, girls— I do too much work for one simple sou— I saw a man die on the gallows today, and I was writing all about it before he was dead."

"Tell us about it," Selma asked quickly.

"Nothing to tell about him dying—except he was too smart to die for a dame."

He held his empty glass out. The maid filled it instantly.

Mother Rosenbloom's eyes danced. The reporter looked at the smiling faces around him and said, "He was a character, girls, he was a character," the reporter hiccoughed. "The warden said to him, 'Now if there's anything I can do for you, let me know.' The warden must be seventy-five; his wife looks older.

"'All right,' says the man who was going to die,—'get me a typewriter and a lot of paper.' They sent the machine and paper down to him.

"He began to write letters to the warden.

"The first one was:

> *Dear Old Pal:*
> *You old screw bum, I'm not going to be long in this world, so I would like for you to do me a favor. Send that old hag of a wife of yours down to share my lonely nights. I'll be nice to her. She's in her second childhood anyhow, and you can't do her any good. Please answer by return guard.*

"The warden nearly died when he got the letter. But what in the hell can you do with a guy you're going to kill anyhow? Even had the old fogy's wife been willing to go, the warden would no doubt have objected."

The tears ran down Mother Rosenbloom's round cheeks as she said, "Men are so damn funny that way."

The reporter began to talk again, as he held his glass for more champagne....

"In a few days the warden gets another letter, 'Listen, you old man-killer,' it said, 'why the hell don't you send that old fuzzy-wuzzy down to me? How would you like to be penned up this way? Is it not a decent Christian thing to make a man's last stay on earth one of bliss? I can't wear the old hag out—you didn't do it in fifty years. Suppose I have killed one woman; that's no sign I'd ever kill another. Besides, the dame I killed burned my toast. Now what the hell would you do in a case like that? So gallop that old nag down to my cell—and I'll show her how a Christian can die—among other things.'

"The warden opened no more letters from the condemned man. But each time one came his face became redder. He could hardly wait for the time to come for the prisoner to die. As he walked with the doctor beside him to the chair, the guy turned and said, 'Say, Warden, I've got something on my mind, and I'd like to have you help me.'

"'What is it?' snapped the warden.

"'Well, sir, I've just been wondering if you spelt c— with a c or a k.'

"The warden allowed the man to die in ignorance." The maid nearly dropped the champagne, as the girls joined her in laughter.

Mother Rosenbloom rocked in glee, and, panting, asked, "Why did they ever kill a man like that?" The doorbell rang.

Judge Slattery and four newspaper men arrived.

Chapter 27

THE lover of the Empress was deserted as the girls gathered about Slattery and the newcomers.

"What the hell's here?" he shouted. Smiling before him was the coffee-colored maid with the champagne.

He gulped another glass and mumbled, "All right, Empress." Leaning his head to one side, he closed his eyes.

The room became animated. Slattery motioned to Leora. She came to him at once.

She noticed the fine texture of his clothes, and Slattery wore them as gracefully as a tiger did its skin. She liked that.

There was in his every movement something akin to the tiger. The touch of his powerful hand sent her blood tingling. She wanted to be near him, and, more than that, she wanted to hear him talk.

Slattery had never married. He had kept his mother until she withered away.

Mother Rosenbloom had talked of him that day.

"He can drink liquor like a funnel, and then whole months pass and he won't touch the stuff. He can get a name in a minute and he never forgets it—and he makes it sound like music—so the person he talks to never forgets.

"They tell a tale about him I'll never believe. They say that when Governor Millard was drunk in the Wilmington Hotel, he called up the penitentiary and asked for Willis, a man they were hanging. The warden told him Willis was to die, and the governor ordered him to the telephone. Millard always hated the judge—and he wasn't satisfied to win over him the only time in sixteen years—he wanted to get him mixed up in something—Anyway, they brought Willis from the death cell, and if there's anything in the story, he proved how loyal the judge's friends are. When the governor said, 'Listen,

Willis—you die tonight—only one thing can save you—whom did you do it for—name him and you're a free man. Remember, you'll be a corpse tomorrow if you don't. Was Slattery back of everything?' The governor waited at the 'phone and then he heard Willis say, 'I don't know what you're talkin' about, Governor; let me die in peace.'"

Mother continued, "Millard was defeated and Willis went in."

All of this went through her mind as she stood close to the great politician and heard him exchange sallies with Selma and the reporters.

Selma was in a high mood. The professor sat at the piano, his hands not moving, while his eyes, slightly bleared, were half closed.

He became more alert as Selma said, "That reminds me of a story about two old maids in the insane asylum."

Eager to hear anything about women who had the effrontery to remain old maids, the girls said in unison, "Do tell it."

"Well," and Selma paused to see that she had the attention of all, "one time two old maids were together in a nut-house for thirty years. Finally one said, 'I wish to to God I had a great big lover who'd just kiss me and love me till I screamed for more. I'm getting sick of this kind of life.'

"Her sister looked at her in surprise for several minutes. 'Now you're talking sense, Sister,' she said. 'If you keep on talking that way they'll let you out of here in another week.'"

All laughed merrily. Leora smiled at the judge.

"That's like the Englishman who intended to start a sporting-house," a reporter for the Argus began, "He said to the other members of his club, 'Well, I think I'll be going into business next week.'

"'What kind of business?' they all asked.

"'A house of prostitution,' he answered.

"'That'll cost you a lot of money—girls come high,' a member said.

"'Oh, no,' said the Englishman. 'I intend to start modestly. I'll use some of my girl friends until we get well started.'"

Mother Rosenbloom's body shook like blubber in mirth.

The maid wheeled a tableful of food and liquor into the parlor.

"Do tell another story, one of you men," said Mother Rosenbloom.

"Would you like one more serious?" asked a reporter, "about mother love, say?"

"Surely, we're all mothers," laughed Mother Rosenbloom, as all the women moved closer to the reporter.

He gulped several times, drained his glass, touched his lips with his tongue and began, "Well—it's about a Hindoo boy who loved a girl too much for his own good, as many men will. He offered her the world, which, strangely enough, being a woman, she did not take—for she wanted something else.

"She hated the boy's mother... 'All I want is your mother's heart,' she said, 'dripping blood from her body.'

"The boy hesitated, as even in those days it was not considered proper to murder one's mother too hurriedly.

"But, after all, he was in love and he consented.

"Within a short time he had murdered his mother and was soon jaunting toward his sweetheart with her heart in a basket.

"Along a rough road he stumbled and fell, face downward in the dust.

"His mother's heart rolled a few feet away from him.

"He heard a voice, as he groaned in pain. It came from his mother's heart, and it asked,

"'Are you hurt, my son?'"

A pause followed.

"That story's older'n God," said James J. Blaidor, rubbing his eyes.

"Shut up, Bladder—if the *Bulletin* had it, they'd give it a headline," the teller of the tale laughed.

"But you've got no right to tell stories like that. How in the hell can a heart talk?"

"In many ways," said Mary Ellen, taking him seriously.

"That's right," put in Doris.

Old or new, the story had touched all the girls but Selma.

Leora moved in surprise. Slattery drew her to him. Mary Ellen looked at the speaker, then at Mother Rosenbloom.

Finally Mother Rosenbloom said, "That's a fine story."

Silence came for a full minute.

To relieve the tension, Selma sang in a mock tone,

> *If I were drowned in the deepest sea,*
> *Mother o' Mine, o Mother o' Mine-*
> *I know whose love would come down to me...*
> *Mother o' Mine, o Mother o' Mine*

Mary Ellen shuddered. "Well, that's enough about mothers. There's no mother story can top that one." "Indeed not," put in Mother Rosenbloom.

Rising from the davenport with difficulty, James J. Blaidor joined the group.

"Let's have a grandmother story— I'll tell you about mine. She was a hundred and eight last month—and we were all talkin' about sex after church, a man and me and a Sunday School teacher, and we all got to wondering how old a person had to be not to enjoy a little get-together party.

"The Sunday School teacher didn't know. She wasn't over seventy, so she asked my grandmother—"Well, Grandma shook her head and says,

"'You've got to ask someone older' n me.'"

Mother Rosenbloom doubled in mirth.

"But that's nothing, folks," resumed James J. Blaidor— "My grandfather was a hundred and forty-seven when he died—it was a tough blow to Grandma—he'd started to church, and took a notion to stop in at Betsy Adal's place where he knew all the girls— They served him a lot of liquor— Finally he takes the oldest battle-ax in the house up stairs—she must have been sixty-four. Anyhow, he got so damn rough with her she had to shoot him."

"Did your grandmother marry again?" asked Judge Slattery.

"Oh yes," was the answer, "a woman like Grandma couldn't stay single long— 'My body needs nourishment,' she used to say—so finally she married a newspaper editor, and inside of two months she was cheating on him."

Chapter 28

The professor pounded the piano until the laughter died away.

James J. Blaidor appreciated the merriment. Stumbling about the room he scowled in the direction of his fellow reporter and chortled, "You and your damn hearts that talk—you stole that story from Longfellow or somebody—maybe it's in the Bible—it's old enough."

"Well it's a damn good yarn, ain't it—and it goes well with women."

"Oh, I don't know—just because you're a guest of the state is no sign you can tell all the old stuff here." Judge Slattery winked.

"But, Jimmy," he said.

"Bladder's his name, Judge. He'd think he was in society if you called him Jimmy."

"What is it, Judge—pay no attention to this riffraff."

"Well, Jimmy, that happened to my grandfather." "No, it happened to mine," volunteered another reporter.

"None of you had grandfathers—you were all hatched out of eggs the cook threw away."

He turned around, "Where's the Empress?"

The colored maid was at his side with the champagne. The glasses were again filled.

The girls drank sparingly.

Judge Slattery moved to a large leather chair. A circle formed around him.

"If you clucks want a story—how about this one?" asked James J. Blaidor—"don't answer, for it won't be funny—

"There was a little girl in England, not over twenty, who was hanged for killing her baby because she wasn't married. She was very pretty, and she sobbed a little before she went to the gallows. 'Come on,' said the hangman, 'poor dear, poor dear—it's God that knows I'd rather sleep with ye than hang ye.'"

"Oh," Mary Ellen gasped.

"The poor little devil," sighed Mother Rosenbloom.

"They'll do anything in England," said Doris Mahone.

"Except to give Ireland a break," hiccoughed James J. Blaidor.

Slattery, whose parents came from Ireland, said nothing.

Their wanton hearts were touched.

"I think that's terrible," said Mary Ellen.

"Why?" asked a reporter, "the kid was better off—and had a better home, maybe, than its mother could have given it."

"But just the same—the girl was a cowardly bitch—what people said was worth more to her than her own baby." Selma was stubborn.

"Perhaps you don't know all the circumstances,"

James J. Blaidor moved closer to her. "Maybe she already had half a dozen—those school-teachers are prolific as hell— They tell me they're good, too—the Empress of Zulu always wanted to teach school until I discouraged her."

Ignoring his mockery, Selma snapped

"Well, just the same, I'd of raised the baby—what the hell's the difference?"

"No, you wouldn't," a reporter said.

"The hell I wouldn't— I'm raising one now—and I'm damned proud of it too."

"That's the girl," said James J. Blaidor— "We'll write an editorial about that in the morning."

"Why do women hate to have babies?" asked Selma. "I knew a girl who had one. She was a young schoolteacher. She didn't want to go through with it so she went to a judge who helped women—and he told her to go ahead and have it and he'd help her out by taking the baby after it was born. By the time the child came, he had a good home for it—the only agreement was that she would never ask about it. She went back to teaching school, and when the child was six years old, it went to be taught by its own mother."

Mother Rosenbloom asked with interest, "Did she find out it was her child?"

"No—and the little girl was her favorite all that term. It went to the same school five years and neither of them ever knew."

James J. Blaidor raised his glass and sang,

> *When I was young, and in my prime,*
> *I had hot knuckles all the time—,*
> *And now I'm old and my joints are sore,*
> *And I can't get hot knuckles any more—*

"God, that's awful," Selma said—"he sings like a raven—anything's better than that— Won't someone tell us another story—about love this time—we all believe in love." Her voice was mocking as she looked at the other girls. "You believe in love, don't you Leora?"

The judge's arm was about her.

"Surely," she answered.

"All right, I'll tell you about a girl in love," said the *Argus* reporter.

There was instant attention.

"She'd been in the hospital.

"One morning she went to the superintendent and asked if she could get out. The superintendent told her she was hardly well enough to go. But when the girl insisted so much the superintendent told her that she might leave.

"The girl was a little street-walker, and she didn't have a dime. She hurried to the little room she'd always had and straightened it up."

"Was she getting ready for business?" asked Selma. "Yes, getting ready for business," responded the reporter.

"Go on," said Leora.

"Yes, do," said Mary Ellen.

"After she'd fixed up, she went down on the street and looked at the different men as they passed. "Finally a man came along. He had a heavy red mustache and little black eyes. He didn't look any too good to the girl, but she needed the money, so she took him up to her room.

"He gave her two dollars.

"She hurried away and bought a bunch of violets; then went out to the cemetery and put them on her sweetheart's grave."

"Well, well," said Mother Rosenbloom.

The reporter waited for further interruptions. None came. He resumed.

"He'd been hanged a year ago that day, and the girl had promised to put flowers on his grave every anniversary.

"When she got back to the room, the landlady said, 'I saw you going up stairs with that man, but I felt you needed the money, so I didn't say anything . . . but really, it's too bad you had to go up with him.'

"'Who was he?' asked the girl.

"'The hangman,' answered the landlady.

"Oh, -my God," gasped Mary Ellen.

Mother Rosenbloom's bosom went up and down. Slattery's eyes

were half closed. Finally he said, "Jesus Christ!" and held Leora closer to him.

Selma whistled softly. Mary Ellen looked at Leora. She had tears in her eyes.

Unconscious as time, James J. Blaidor had stretched himself on the davenport.

"Now choose your girls," said Judge Slattery.

A reporter put his arms on Leora's shoulders. She drew back against the judge, saying half shyly, "Please, I don't want to go."

"Why not?" asked the reporter. "You're not married, are you?"

"Yes," was Leora's answer.

Soon the different couples went up stairs. Slattery made no move.

"We'll talk here a while," he said to Leora.

Mother Rosenbloom motioned to the professor and left discreetly. The professor played lower and lower. Soon his hands stopped on the keys. He, too, had gone from the room.

No word was said between Slattery and the girl. She clung to him like a frightened child for fear she would fall from his lap.

Not talkative the whole evening, he now sat in complete silence.

Leora tried to snuggle closer to him. He did not move.

She remained quiet for some time, and then, her feeling overcoming her, she ran her hand through his hair. Still there was no response.

Remaining still for the second time, she held her hand over his heart and counted the even beats for a few seconds.

She could feel his arms holding her. For the first time in her life, every fibre of her body was relaxed. Suddenly she heard the clamour of a couple coming down the stairs. She jumped from the judge's lap and kissed him lingeringly on the mouth.

As Selma and the reporter for the Argus reached the parlor, Leora said, "My, it takes you people a long time."

"Yes, Kid, I had an old man," Selma returned banteringly.

"Not so damned old," laughed the reporter.

When the time came to go, James J. Blaidor was carried to the car.

"I hope you didn't treat the Empress this way," Mary Ellen nudged him.

"The poor Empress—and you're the one who was going to wear us all out," Selma pinched his cheeks. James J. Blaidor's head sagged. He made no answer.

In leaving, Judge Slattery caressed Leora lightly, and placed a bill in her hand.

She tried to hand it back. He said decisively, "You mustn't."

When all had gone, Doris asked, "Did he disappoint you?"

"Not at all," answered Leora— "How could he?" Still holding the money, Leora went to her room. It was a hundred dollar note.

She went to Mother Rosenbloom with the bill. "I owe you fifty," she said.

Mother Rosenbloom looked at the money. "No you don't," was her decision.

Long that night she lay and thought. Was he really fond of her? She did not know. Oblivious of everything else, she could feel his arms around her.

The professor brought several letters to Leora next evening. As always, she opened Sally's letter first. Buddy had come home and was now at work as a switch-tender in the railroad yards.

Denny was so proud of his new suit, and often talked of his sister. He had passed a store with Sally. Seeing a wax model in the window wearing an evening gown and a fur coat he pointed and shouted, so that passersby could hear— "Look, Sally, Leora's one of them."

Sally took his hand and hurried him away, while he continued to look backward at the model.

Leora closed the letter with a smile.

Money had made so much difference in her father's house, and her broken-down mother was not there to enjoy it. With the heritage of the sensitive poor, a feeling of belligerency took possession of her.

It passed as she opened the next letter. It was from Dr. Farway.

She opened it slowly and looked at the certified check for a hundred dollars that it contained. She folded it several times and mused before reading the letter. It had all been like something that happened to some one else.

Her quick mind compared him with Slattery. She knew the difference without being able to explain it to herself. Slattery "just was" as Selma had said.

She began to read Dr. Farway's letter. "You've been gone about two years," it said, "and it seems like five."

And then, as though it were something he had just remembered, "Mrs. Farway died nearly two weeks ago. We had many differences, as you know, and even though she could not bear the child I so much wanted, I am lost without her." . . .

Leora did not read the letter to the end. She had the impulse to telephone to Alice, and then dismissed it. The thought came to her, "Why can't I go back and marry him if Mary Ellen intends to marry her lawyer?" She shuddered at the thought of leaving Slattery.

A bell rang. The maid knocked at her door and said, "Ladies in the parlor." Leora answered, "All right," but did not move.

In a few minutes another knock came. It was the housekeeper. Mother Rosenbloom would like to see her.

Mother was not yet dressed. In its fluffs and laces, her enormous body looked twice as large. Her pink silk nightgown had a dainty lace yoke and no sleeves. Her arms, large as the legs of a man, were bare.

"Judge Slattery telephoned, Leora," she said, as a maid finished waving her hair. "He wants you to be at the Randolph Hotel at ten tonight."

"Why, Mother?" Leora gasped.

"I'm sure he likes you or he wouldn't send for you like this."

"But, Mother—I'm so—"

"No, don't be anything but yourself, and don't tell him how to run the state—more women get no place by talking too much than anything else."

She rang the bell.

"Bring Selma and Mary Ellen to me."

The maid bowed.

"Too bad that girl's high yellow. She's got more brains than most women," said Mother Rosenbloom. It was the same maid who had kept James J. Blaidor's glass full.

When Selma and Mary Ellen arrived, Mother said to them, "Leora's meeting Judge Slattery tonight—help her dress, girls."

When the girls entered Leora's room, they found her in a clinging blue velvet dress. It made the blue of her eyes more vivid, and turned the rich brown of her hair to copper.

Slattery had sent her a corsage of gardenias.

Selma gasped, "My God—you know what to wear all right."

Mary Ellen ran her hand over the curve of Leora's breasts. "No wonder he fell for you," she said. Leora smiled in the mirror.

The girls returned with Leora.

Mother Rosenbloom looked at her and said, "Lovely." "What's going on, Mother?" asked Selma.

"Some gathering—the judge doesn't want to be alone."

The girls were soon on their way to the Randolph.

"I've got a hunch," said Selma, "I believe you're in." She sighed, "I'd give my right eye for a man like him." The cab turned a corner and swayed Selma toward Leora. "Damn, you do look lovely," she said, adjusting herself—"I can understand the whole thing."

"Why?" asked Leora.

"Just one of those things—you're in—that's all."

The cab stopped at the hotel.

"We'll wait here," Selma commanded the driver. Slattery's man was standing at the entrance.

He stepped forward and took Leora through the crowded lobby and up the elevator to the Blue Room. It was really a penthouse and overlooked the city.

In the room were politicians, pugilists, gangsters, lawyers, and people from the different theatres.

Arm in arm with Judge Slattery, a great criminal lawyer leaned against the bar. A famous actor had just introduced him as the leading member of the American Bar Association. When Leora entered, the applause had not died down. She was taken to Slattery. The judge greeted her warmly and introduced her to the lawyer. Soon a tall man with a hooked nose joined them. "Miss La Rue—may I present the governor—Governor Harris—Miss La Rue—"

The governor bowed politely.

Hours passed. There was dancing and music. The governor made an address. Men and women gathered about the governor and Slattery when it came time to go.

Judge Slattery's car waited at the main entrance. With the governor and the great criminal lawyer, the famous actor and others, Leora was taken to his home.

The men treated her with the utmost consideration.

After they had been at his home for an hour or more, the judge said to her, "I think you had better retire, Leora."

It was the first time he had spoken her name.

A maid appeared and escorted her to an elegantly furnished room.

She awoke late.

The judge joined her at breakfast.

"I leave for New York at once," he said. "I'll take you home on the way to the station."

"Did you have a nice time?" he asked, as the car went toward Mother Rosenbloom's.

"Oh, so nice," she said impulsively, putting a delicately gloved hand on his forearm.

"That's good. I thought you would enjoy it. The governor and I were hungry boys together."

"I don't know how to thank you." Leora leaned toward him—"It meant so much to me."

"Don't," he said, "it's all right,—I'll be back in a week— Mother will talk to you."

He rang the bell for her.

"Good-bye— In a week," he said.

In another moment he was in the limousine.

Mother Rosenbloom was having her coffee and reading the newspapers when Leora entered.

She asked with the same solicitude as Judge Slattery, "Did you have a nice time?"

"So nice," Leora answered. "He's grand."

"The judge talked to me last night," Mother Rosenbloom confided, motioning Leora to sit on her bed. "He wants you to stay on here with me—I'll have the bookkeeper figure what you've earned the past month—you'll be paid your half of that—and see no other men."

Mother studied a report.

"I'll go fifty-fifty with you on liquor—that should get you another hundred a week anyhow—will that please you?"

"Yes, Mother," answered Leora. "I never want to see another man."

"That's good—the judge will take care of everything." Smiling, she added, "He said a nice thing about you over the telephone."

"What, Mother?"

"That you weren't silly—and so respectful." "Who wouldn't be, Mother?"

Mother did not answer the question. Instead, she turned her newspaper to the society page and looked at the pictures of several society women in riding costumes.

"They're bigger whores than us," she growled, turning the page hastily.

Looking at Leora, she said, "Now, dear—you can explain to the girls—they'll understand."

Before Leora reached the door, Mother added, "You're much better off—the patent on men won't wear out—or on women either—it's grand to think he likes you—but I knew he would the minute you came into the house—I'll explain it to you some day—maybe."

Chapter 29

Events came rapidly for Leora. On the third night she received a long distance telephone call. After Slattery had talked to her he said, "Put Mother on the 'phone."

When Mother had finished, she smiled, "He wants us to wire him at the Willard in Washington. He's still a lonesome little boy—did he tell you?" she asked.

Leora, still agitated over the long distance call, nodded, "Yes."

"Now send him a nice telegram," said Mother. "You won't have to lie—you do miss him—*I know*."

Leora spent some time in wording the telegram. The gruff matchmaker looked at it and asked, "Where's the one you wrote first?"

Mother looked it over. "It's the best—I knew it would be. Anything from the heart is never studied." She rang for Mary Ellen.

"You're more patient than me, Mary Ellen—and Leora might get too excited. Telephone these telegrams for us."

Mary Ellen picked up Mother's receiver and with clear articulation read the messages. When she came to the end of Leora's she pronounced the words, "All my love," as though her own heart were in them. They sounded strange to Leora. She had never written such words to anyone but Sally and her aunt before.

More men selected Leora in the next few days than ever before.

"They're like dogs," Mother said grimly, "they know."

The women in the house, from Mother Rosenbloom to the cook, treated Leora with new deference. Whether due to Mother's training or the innate largeness of spirit in Selma, Mary Ellen, and Doris, they exhibited a kindly envy without jealousy.

"It's nice of him not wanting her with other men," observed Selma.

"Tut, tut,"—said Mother, "it's not nice at all—he's a man—and he doesn't want to share."

"Maybe he thinks it'll turn into a maidenhead again," said Doris.

"Where did you learn that—in the reform school?" Mother asked.

When the judge returned, Mother sent Leora to meet him several times in different sections of the city. It was generally at a public function or dinner. Treated with respect, she would be returned to Mother Rosenbloom after a light caress.

At times Slattery would talk to her, but always in short sentences.

When she had said, "Governor Harris has such sad eyes, hasn't he?" Slattery replied,

"Yes,—they come from indigestion."

"Why is Mother so fond of you?" Leora asked him. "She's getting old," he said.

"But she's still very smart," was Leora's retort. "That's why she likes me," returned Slattery. Another month passed when word came to Mother from Slattery to have Leora find an apartment. Alice could help her.

Leora cried for joy as Mother told her. She hurried to telephone Alice.

"Now remember—nothing garish—you've seen his house," Mother warned.

For several days the girls looked at apartments until they located one on a top floor. The windows of the living-room overlooked the lake. While Alice bargained, Leora watched the vast white and blue body of water and saw a ship, far out, going, she wondered where.

"Would you like this one, Leora?" Alice asked.

"I'd love it—I could spend hours at this window." "Then we'll take it," said the business-like Alice. On their way to Mother Rosenbloom's, Alice said to her cousin, "Now if the judge disappears for a few days, it'll be because he's drinking. He snaps out of it in three days—and Mr. Everlan told me it came over him about every month—but he's always kind.—I've seen him that way—"

"I don't care what he does," Leora assured Alice, "I love him."

"How changed you are," observed Alice.

The professor brought a letter from Farway. He asked Leora to return and marry him.

She started to write to him at once—to tell him that she loved another man. Then she hesitated. Instead, she talked it over with Alice.

"Tell him you want time to consider," was her advice. For the next week Leora was like a bride, selecting, with Alice, the furniture for the apartment.

When all was ready in the new home, the desire for drink came over Slattery.

Accompanied by Alice and Mr. Everlan, he came to Mother Rosenbloom's in a heavy rainstorm.

The door banged open after they entered the parlor. A gust of wind swept in. Raindrops rattled loudly against the window panes.

"What a night," exclaimed Mother Rosenbloom, "it would drown a duck."

The rattle of the rain and the crash of thunder dimmed the professor's music.

Though sex was still for sale, there were no buyers on such a night.

Leora came into the parlor with Selma and ran to Slattery's arms. Mary Ellen and Doris followed.

Several hours of merrymaking passed. Mother Rosenbloom accompanied the professor at the piano.

The rain could be heard splashing during the intervals of merriment.

During a silence Alice looked at her wrist-watch and said to Mother Rosenbloom, "We must be going soon."

"What," exclaimed Mother, "on such a night—you'll need a boat."

The judge looked at Mr. Everlan, "No, old pal, you're not going—and leave me alone here with all these women—why I would never forgive you."

Mr. Everlan hesitated.

"Why dear me, no," said Mother Rosenbloom. "Your driver is sound asleep. You would be drowned getting to the car." Mother Rosenbloom looked sternly at Alice, "*You must stay.*"

"All right, Mother," returned Alice obediently. "Pour us all a drink," commanded the judge. "I'll do it, Mother," said Leora.

When another hour had passed, Mother Rosenbloom said, "Well, I think I'll retire." She looked at her guests. "Now please stay until morning and maybe the rain will let up—you and Mr. Everlan take the end room, Alice."

The judge and Mr. Everlan rose.

A maid followed Mother Rosenbloom to her rooms. When all had gone, Leora held Slattery's hand. "I think we had better go too," she suggested.

"All right," the judge said, rising, "We will have liquor sent to the room."

Leora led him to her room.

A knock came at the door.

The maid placed liquor on a small serving table.

She placed an arm about him, kissed him quickly and said, "I'll be so happy in the lovely apartment overlooking the lake—and I'll love you so."

His hand went along the curve of her body. She helped him to the bed.

"Now be a good boy and lie here just a moment while I put on a robe," she said, placing her hands upon his shoulders and pressing him backward. "I'm not leaving you," she soothed.

His head was on the pillow. She stroked his hair. He breathed deeply.

"Don't leave me," he said.

His hand bent her body to him.

She kissed his eyes.

"Get me some liquor, Leora," he said.

She brought it to him at once.

"I'm sorry for this," his voice was soft.

"You don't need to be."

"You mean that?" He emptied the glass.

"From the bottom of my heart," was her reply. "Do you really like me?" he asked.

"I love you."

"Do you tell them all that?"

"You're the only one I've ever ,told that." Her voice was full of candor.

"Well, it's a good story." He asked for more liquor.

"Yes, I knew you'd say that," she bit her lip

"Now I want to be honest with you," she said. He remained quiet while she told the story of her life. After she had finished telling of the two seductions, he said, "Well, the moon's as far from both of us—I didn't expect to find you a virgin, and neither did I expect this."

"But it's my nature," Leora explained, "I've got to play square when I love."

"Oh well," he smiled, "don't worry about a few seductions—I'd rather have had you first, but I can't be everywhere at once—we can't change things, even if we try until the stars fall."

He asked for more liquor.

"I've wanted you so much," went on Leora, "and when I have you alone here with me you've been drinking too much."

Jim Tully

"Not too much," responded Slattery. "My head's clear—I've wanted you before—but I don't dare get too excited—" he stopped, "maybe it's better to go out in a blaze."

"You do need me, don't you?" Leora huddled close to him—"I'd like to be just your slave—I'd wait on you all the time—I'd give you everything I had—everything —Mother Rosenbloom once told me you could charm a bird out of a tree, even if a cat was waiting for it—won't you let me be your bird?—Do say you need me—do saybe so happy."

He pulled her closer. "Yes, I do need you—very much—I'm a very lonely man—a very, very lonely man—"

His tone of voice changed.

"It's funny how we need people," he said, reaching for the glass. "Here I'm a horse, and I lean on a lovely fly like you—but it's all in fun," he sighed, with an effort at banter, and was calm a moment before he resumed, "Just stand by me, dearie—just you and me.

"They can't make a law in this state without me, dear. I put them in and I take them out—and believe me—I know what it's all about. I made Jack Harris governor just like that." Leora heard his fingers snap. "And I'll tell you why—he was good to me when I was a kid… He was a Jew boy, and the Jews and the Micks have always been pals. My mother gave me twenty cents, and Harris and I were going to the bootjacks to get our papers. We stopped in an alley to shoot craps with two Niggers and a Wop kid, and I won eighty cents and the two Nigger kids beat me up and took the eighty cents and my twenty cents besides. Well, Harris and the Wop kid began to battle, and they knocked the Niggers out, and got my dollar back, and they didn't take a nickel that belonged to the Nigger kids—'Thanks,' I said, 'Jackie,' and he said, 'Don't thank me, you little Mick—let's go and get our papers or your ma and mine'll knock the living hell out of us'—and so we all three went and got our papers— That's been thirty-four years ago.

"By the time I was twenty-three I owned a saloon—and had my hands on a dozen houses like this. My pal, Harris, the Jew boy, went in for books and studied law—I didn't give a damn about books… it was people I liked. What the hell can any book tell me about people? I'm forty-eight years old and I run a state—and I can't dig a girl like you out of a book."

As a reward for the compliment, Leora pressed her lips against his mouth. He took the kiss with a sigh, and went on, "Harris is all the time spouting things to me, but when he wants anything done fast he comes to me.

It was me who made him state senator, then a congressman, and a governor. I tell him what to say to people to make them love him—for you've got to love people if you want them to love you back... you've got to be willing in your soul to share all you've got, if you steal it back the next minute. It's give and take, around and around, like a drunken dollar whore on a merry-go-round—that's what life is, and don't never let them tell you any different

"Harris said to me after I put him in as governor, 'You Irish always have a salamander in your heart—' and I asked him what the hell a salamander was and he said—'a lizard the fire can't burn,'—and I said,'Jack—that's because we're smart—no matter how hot we seem there's a cold place in our heads and hearts.'" The judge laughed aloud. "'Damn you,' Jack said, 'you've always got an answer.'—'Sure, Jack—don't you know it—my answer to politics is you—where do you think I came from, Jack—I've got a noodle too—just because I don't think with dead men's thoughts out of books is no reason I'm not smart—I'm barroom smart, Jack, and that's the smartest kind—you can't lift your left eyelid without me knowing what you're thinking'

"And by God, I've done good in this world—I've done favors for every bum I ever knew who was white, and a hell of a lot who weren't—Mother Rosenbloom can tell you—and so can Everlan. I started from scratch, I did—nobody was too mean for me to know—and when Harris got to be a lawyer and went in a corporation office, and I'd begun to feel my way in politics in my ward, and knew that I had it sewed up tight as a poorhouse shroud, I said to Jack, 'You and me are a great combination, a Mick and a Yid—but you've got to give some of your time to people—you've got to get up in court and defend bums and thieves and murderers—for you and me's going places... I'll make you the first Jew president— Now read your books at home and don't mention them—when you see Biddy Flaherty, you must talk to her about her kid's bellyache from eating the green apples—and things like that—and be kind to everybody you see, for they've all got tongues, and they can all be sharp no matter how dull their heads are.'"

"I think you're grand," Leora said with conviction.

"None of that now—give me liquor."

She quickly poured him another glass.

"I'm not so wonderful—but I never had any fear—the man without fear can step from cloud to cloud and play handball with the stars—that is—if he can reach them."

In wonder she asked, "Why are you here— You could get all the beautiful women in the world."

"That's simple—these are my people—they're all I've ever known. Mother's got better judgment than the governor—and more brains—if she were a man she'd be President—"

He smiled sardonically, "You're too young to know that all life's a whorehouse—the difference is only that it's not as public as this." He pointed toward the door.

"There's more blackmail out there and less charm. A girl in a house like this never double-crosses a man until she takes a notion to reform. Anything may be done to a fellow in a house, but that's as far as it goes—besides, it's all I know... all I've ever known—and the more I see of life, it's all I ever want to know. I know what to expect when I stay where I belong, and the only thing that makes me proud is that the people who kicked me around when I was a kid now take orders from me. The whole business of living's a long disease—and I'd like to know what the hell more any man can have than a girl like you in bed—and when we have our little hour all we do is make brats for future undertakers and tombstone makers..."

He stopped talking, half rose, and looked in the direction of the liquor. Leora poured a drink for him. He drank it rapidly and sank again on the pillow. "I've never talked to anybody like this before," he said. "That's why I'm for you—damn a woman you can't talk to."

The rain rattled heavily on the roof. The windows shook with the wind and were turned yellow by the lightning.

Water splashed more heavily.

The lightning came in long, jagged and vivid flashes.

He became incoherent for a moment, and then said firmly, "I had a dream last night, Leora. I walked through a street the color of slate pencils, and the rain fell in silver drops as long as an old woman's dream. I went up to the Masonic Temple Building and I said to myself, 'I'm going to kill all the damned people inside.' So I crushed it in my fingers and shook it like a cat would a mouse—it was awful, the twisted iron girders and the broken brick and mortar. I suddenly felt sorry and I stooped down to pick up all the hurt people who fell out of the building. They didn't look like grown-ups any more, but just children—and suddenly I grew so tall I couldn't stoop low enough to touch them . . . so I left them all lying in the street and went out to find a sack of star dust—then I was arrested for murder.

"When I stood up to get my sentence, the judge looked at me with daggers in his eyes. 'He had no mercy,' he said, 'neither have I.'

"The first thing I knew a fellow about thirty, with a long cloak and a Van Dyke beard and sad eyes and curly red hair, stood by me... and he said to the judge, with a voice like music,

I told him I was weak as a rained-on bee—
I told him I was lost—He said, 'Lean on me.'

"'And who are you?' asked the judge.

"'My name is Christ—I came a long distance. I live in the mountains behind the moon. I beseech you not to hang this man—he already has imagination, and that is punishment enough.'

"Another man pointed to the red-headed man and said, 'This is the justest man that ever the sun shone on.'

"And the judge said, 'Get the hell out of here, all of you—this is a court of law. Take your justice to the mountains behind the moon.'

"As we left the courtroom, I could hear them pounding the nails in the gallows, and one guard yelled out, 'Make that rope bigger and stronger, you can't break this fellow's neck with an inch rope—he's a politician.'

"'We don't give a damn what he is, we'll pop his neck like a bottle of champagne,' another guard yelled. 'He's not satisfied to bump one man. He took a building full of people anxious to earn an honest living, and he sprawled them out on the street like a lot of dead butterflies...

"All the way to the gallows the people hissed at me—they were the same people I couldn't pick up because I'd grown so tall—I stumbled as I looked up and saw the rope—and then I woke up"

Footsteps were heard.

"It's Mother, seeing that everything is all right," said Leora.

"What a woman," the judge said. "Her brain's as big as her body. Whenever I'm stuck about what to do in the Capitol, I go to her. She's the way people should be in this world—hard as a rock and soft as a baby—you should have seen her twenty years ago—just as smart as now—born smart. She just knew and never had to learn."

"Where did Mother come from?" Leora asked with assumed innocence.

The judge's hand moved up and down her body before he answered softly, "That's not for little girls to know. Mother's always been here, protecting us poor men from the rain and the cold. I think she came from a cloud hundreds of years ago. She was the greatest friend I had when everything was dark as the back of a Nigger's ear—I was a young fellow then, and just as sure as God put worms in big apples I'd be the President of the United States by now if it hadn't happened—they got the goods on me, and I had to step behind the curtains—to play back of the scenes—

"Mother was big time even then—when I had to right-about-

Jim Tully

face and shift my whole career, she said to me, —'You're the biggest man in the state—pull the strings, you'll get more fun out of it'

"But anyhow—they were voting on liquor as they always are in this God-damned country, but this time the legislature had the vote. I packed it with men to make it even anyhow. I thought I had the brewers and the distillers eating out of my hand, and two hundred thousand on the side—we'd polled the whole business, when one of the members died down state, and I had to hurry there and get another one in we could control, and by God he balked, and I began to work on him in the Vaner Hotel—he was a hick who wouldn't stay put—so he tipped the other side off and they dictaphoned the room. It was a new thing then; we hushed it all up by letting them win—but I was never allowed to come out in the open again. So I picked on Harris—and now I sit back and watch him get the glory, when I could have held high office and do all that I'm doing anyhow."

Leora move uneasily. She had never felt the same before.

The politician's white silk shirt was open at the throat. His expensive scarf was loose. He looked upward with half-closed eyes. His mouth was closed tight. A dent was on each side of his jaw. His face might have been chiseled out of marble.

Leora leaned over, her breasts pressed firmly against him. She who was without his terrifying strength wanted to protect him, to hold him in her arms forever.

She could hear his heart beat as she snuggled closely to him. Then suddenly she kissed him passionately again and again.

She then removed her clothes and lay quiet, expectant, beside him.

His touch burned her body.

She half swooned under his embrace.

Moments of wild delirium followed. Every particle of her body responded in ecstatic rhythm.

When all was over, she held him close for a long time, forgetful of everything. Not a word was spoken. Soon she heard his regular deep breathing.

Resting on her elbow, she gazed at him, then snapped the small light by the bed, and laid contentedly beside him.

Chapter 30

Her mind and heart in turmoil, she remained long without moving. The awakening had been so tremendous, she was still bewildered. She had never dreamed that such a thing were possible, and here she lay, her body still on fire, and ready to cross the world for one man.

The thought came that she might be with child. She hoped it were correct—she would have it no matter what happened. To have a child by him—at last she realized how her mother felt about children. Surely her mother had never been so deeply stirred.

She hoped that he would always love her. The thought of another man, at any price, made her shudder. She wanted to sing, to laugh, to cry.

She covered him gently and resumed her pleasant revery.

If she had a child, and it was a boy—she would call it Brandon—and if it were a girl—she thought of different names. If the judge would not let her have it, she would run away until after it was born—then let Sally have it and come back to him. She wanted the baby and she wanted him.

The rain continued to rattle on the roof, softly, then harder and harder, like the professor's hands going rapidly over the piano keys.

She would write to Dr. Farway in the morning. It had been so long since she had seen him—nearly two years.

She would soon be twenty-one. For a moment she was homesick.

Then, with a full heart, her thoughts returned to the man at her side.

At last her mind quit racing. She dozed. She awoke with a start.

The judge's arm rested heavily upon her. She tried to move it cautiously. The elbow did not bend. She touched his hand. It was still warm, but stiff. Her hand went to his heart.

It was still.

She sat erect for a moment, and rubbed her eyes. In an instant she turned on the lights.

The judge's head was buried in the pillow. His mouth was open. His eyes stared straight upward.

Her eyes too paralyzed for tears, she fell across him for a moment in a daze, then kissed the dead mouth and choked her sobs in the pillow beside him.

Like the jab of a needle in her brain, the clock struck three. She stood erect, her hair down, her slender body, unmindful of the chilled room, uncovered except for the coat of a suit of silk pajamas.

She knelt at the bed beside him, her hands going up and down his arm.

A mist came to her eyes. She wiped them with the sheet. Hurrying to the closet, she put on the other half of the pajamas, a fur coat, and slippers.

She stood for a second in the middle of the room. A clap of thunder roared down the sky.

The windows shook as the rain fell harder against them. The wind whistled and was silenced by louder thunder. Wild flares of lightning turned yellow the water running down the windows.

She left the room quietly and went to Mother Rosenbloom. The large lady lay in a flesh-colored and beribboned nightgown. Her reading lamp, which she had forgotten to turn off, threw a light across the bed.

"What is it, Leora?" Mother asked.

"The judge is dead," she whispered.

The bed sagged in the middle as Mother Rosenbloom sat up suddenly and exclaimed tersely, *"My God, how do you know?"*

"I felt his heart," answered Leora.

The rain still swished against the windows.

"Wake Mr. Everlan up—but not the chauffeur yet," said Mother Rosenbloom.

She hurried from the bed and put on a satin robe. "Let's go to him," she commanded.

Leora followed.

She immediately felt the judge's heart, then his pulse. "You go ahead, Leora, open the front door—then wake Mr. Everlan."

Leora hurried forward.

The mammoth woman took the body of the judge, pulled the legs and arms together, and threw it across her shoulder. The rain fell in cycles white as silver in the street as Leora opened the door.

With set jaws, the woman moved with her burden toward the limousine at the curb. The rain whipped upon them as Mother Rosenbloom held the corpse and Leora opened the car door.

In another second, Mother placed the body erect in the rear seat.

Shutting the car door carefully, she followed Leora into the house.

Bedraggled with rain, her thin clothing plastered to her huge body, the giant woman fell on the davenport and sobbed. Controlling herself long enough to say, "Run and wake Mr. Everlan, dear," she sobbed again.

Then, with a mighty effort, she followed Leora.

Alice came to the door.

"Let me in, dear—something has happened." Mother Rosenbloom stepped inside.

Shaking the sleeping man, she said in a hoarse whisper, "Judge Slattery's dead—I have put him in your car—you must leave here without Alice—I'll wake the chauffeur… he must not know. I'll tell him that you and the judge wish to go to your home. You can discover he has died of heart trouble on the way."

The chauffeur sat stiffly in his seat, while Mr. Everlan said, "The judge and I wish to go to my home, Joe."

The car moved forward through the rainy night.

The three stood in silence.

Mother reached out her arms and drew the girl to her. "I'm so sorry for you, dear," she said to Leora.

"Don't mind me now—you're dripping wet," Leora said to Mother Rosenbloom. "Come, we must put some warm clothes on you."

She put her fur coat over Mother Rosenbloom's shoulders. Shivering, she followed Alice and Leora to her own room.

The girls rubbed her body with towels and put her into bed.

The clock struck four.

There came a dying rumble of thunder. The rain stopped.

The morning papers announced that Judge Slattery, famous political boss of the _____ Ward, had died suddenly of heart trouble while riding with his lifelong friend, J. Whitlau Everlan, the distinguished financier.

His funeral, attended by the governor, was one of the largest ever held in the state. Rich and poor crowded about his bier for a long last look at him.

Young boys sang,

*Under the wide and starry sky,
Dig the grave and let me lie,
Glad did I live and gladly die,
And I laid me down with a will.*

*This be the verse you grave for me;
Here he lies where he longed to be;
Home is the sailor, home from sea,
And the hunter home from the hill.*

Leora left with Alice.

An ancient beggar stood outside the church.

"It doesn't seem right," said Alice. "He was so full of life—and this—" She looked at the beggar.

Leora, her eyes in a mist, said quickly, "He didn't gladly die—I know better." She held her cousin's arm and sobbed, "Oh, Alice!"

The governor met the reporters at the door of the church. His face was the color of a weather-beaten nut. His mouth, at the edges of which were sly quirks of humor, now drooped.

He removed the gold spectacles from his hawk-like nose. Years of success had given him poise. One would not have suspected that as a lad he had shot dice in an alley.

He looked casually about the throng as though expecting a photographer. When several appeared, he posed for a picture. He then said, in a tone of deep affection, and with careful and slow enunciation,

"I will walk silently in his great shadow all the rest of my days. In him were personified the purest and most unselfish of American ideals. He wanted no office for himself. He believed in service to the common good, and now, he lies before us, silent as an empty house through which the wind has blown. Knowing him better than most men, I saw his soul and heart in motion. He would stop to pat the noses of cold horses on the street. I have seen the tears come to his eyes when a beggar passed. I recall as a young man when we were both in deep struggle to find money for ourselves and others that he at last managed to pay forty dollars for an overcoat. It was a staggering price. It was a blue chinchilla and it had a velvet collar, and when we went to dinner together, which cost fifty cents each, he placed the coat on a hook, and upon leaving the restaurant we found that someone had stolen it. Weeks of effort had gone into the getting of that coat, but when the proprietor assured him that he knew the man who had stolen it, and that he could send the police and arrest him, my great friend, who now lies silent forever, said, 'No, no—how badly he must have needed that coat to take the chance of going to jail to steal it—let him have it—I'll get another one.'

The governor of the state paused and wiped the nose-glasses in hand.

"We came," he went on, "out of the sludge of life together. Even as a boy he was cruel as the lash of a whip toward all injustice. Like all of us who try to pierce the veil, he often lost his way, but somehow or other he would find it out of the forest of despair by the light in his own soul. And I venture to say that tonight at hearthstones simple and grand many a heart will ache for the great comrade who has gone on the far and outward trail. He will live in men's hearts until time becomes a hollow echo."

"Will Judge Slattery's death have any effect on the policy of his party?" a reporter asked.

"None whatever," replied the governor, "except as a great memory." He hesitated, "But of course the Democratic Party will ever strive to perpetuate his unflinching love of duty, and his high ideals."

The governor entered his limousine. The reporters wrote swiftly.

James J. Blaidor finished his writing first. "This is a lot of bologna," he said, "but by God, he was a great guy."

Chapter 31

Mother Rosenbloom did not attend the funeral. She was ill with pneumonia. For days she tossed on her bed while doctors and nurses came and went silently.

No word was said to the men who came in search of sex. Business went on as usual. Mother would not have it otherwise.

"I'll whip this thing," she would wheeze. "Just leave it to Mother."

The secretary came at the appointed time and received the earnings from the housekeeper.

The professor played music more softly, and if a guest asked about Mother he was told that she had a slight headache.

She had apparently gained strength on the eighth day.

The girls were allowed to gather for a half hour in her room.

"Why, I'm not leaving you yet, girls. I still have work to do."

The nurse wanted to remove her rings. She would not allow her.

She put a hand on Leora, and said in a whisper, "We did our best, dear."

"How strong you are, Mother," responded Leora. "The poor man," said Mother. "What did it all mean —for a day or two I thought I'd be seeing him soon."

"I wish I could," said Leora.

Mother's eyes roved over the ceiling.

"Why did I have to carry him out?" she asked herself. "Nothing could have hurt him ever again." She breathed heavily.

"But he'd have done it for me. I remember once before he had a heart attack—and he quit drinking for a year—he was a wild man, but his heart was gold. You'll never know, dear, how good a man he was—he'd have given you the sun on a winter day and have stayed in the shade himself."

Mother adjusted the sheet over her enormous breasts, and fought for breath.

"It's all so strange, Leora—here I am, dealing in women like cattle—and only one man has ever been in my life—a pure old virgin—*for him.*"

Mother's barrel body stiffened for a moment and then relaxed. Her hand closed over Leora's.

"It was a long time ago," she said. "He's a shadow I can never get out from under." Her voice went to a whisper, "And there was a boy who looked like him—he's gone too—and here I am—a withered old tree waiting for the ax."

She tried to touch Leora's reddish-brown hair, and sighed deeply.

"But, Mother," said Leora, "you'll be with us a long time yet."

"You mustn't tell funny stories." Mother smiled wanly. "You can't fool Mother—I can hear the birds calling across the river, and all they keep saying is 'Come home, come home.'"

There was a slightly longer silence before Mother said, "The poor judge—I never thought he would go like other men—"

She smiled at Leora, "And in bed with a beauty like you—dear, dear."

"But I loved him, Mother."

"I know, dear—so did I—and everybody. He was the biggest tree in the woods, and even the birds loved him."

Mother's eyes half closed in thought, "And to think he's like me—he leaves nothing behind—not a drop of his own great blood left in the world."

"Mother—" whispered Leora—"*I have his baby.*"

Mother opened her eyes, "You have his what?"

"His baby, Mother—I could feel him in my womb."

"Thank God," said Mother, "that's all you'll ever need." She lay back on the pillow.

Mary Ellen and Selma entered timidly.

Mother made an effort to smile.

After some moments, she whispered, "You girls must always be friends."

They answered in unison, "Yes, Mother."

When Doris came into the room, Mother held a hand toward her. She went to the bed, put a hand on Leora's shoulder, and held Mother's hand with the other.

Mother tried to talk again. The nurse entered and bade her be silent.

The house doctor came into the room, his huge body panting. Mother looked at him and smiled wearily, "It's not a case for you, Doctor."

Doris laughed outright, and held her hand to her mouth. The other girls smiled.

The doctor whispered.

The nurse held up her hand for silence, while Mother fought for breath.

The nurse touched Leora gently. Followed by the house doctor, she and the girls left the room.

Mother held her head far back, and closed her eyes. Like the exhausts of steam from an engine, her breathing became hard and sharp.

All but the house doctor went to Leora's room.

Judge Slattery's picture was still on the dresser. "He's gone, and she's going," Leora sobbed a moment.

"You mustn't," said Mary Ellen, putting an arm about her.

"I'll telephone for Alice," said Leora.

"Let me do it, Leora." Selma left the Loom.

Mother became weaker on the ninth day. In an effort to breathe, she moved her mountainous breasts furiously up and down.

An oxygen apparatus was hurried into her room. "It looks like the last curtain," she gasped.

The priest came. Gentle as the dew and silent as an executioner, he delivered the extreme unction. She breathed more easily. Suddenly, she breathed no more. It was two in the afternoon. She had pushed her hand outside the covers. The sun threw a slant of light upon her many diamonds.

A hush came over the house.

The professor, who had only left the house to get the mail since Mother's illness, received the news of her death with a gulp. He sat silent a long time, his elbows on his knees, his face in his hands. Mary Ellen soothed him for a moment. Neither said a word.

Mother Rosenbloom was removed to an exclusive funeral parlor.

A wide purple crape was placed on the door, through which she had carried Brandon Slattery.

Chapter 32

WHEN the news of Mother Rosenbloom's death went about the city, many men and women called. All were directed to the funeral parlor.

The church was crowded on the day her funeral was held.

She lay in an immense oak coffin, with heavy silver handles, in the same spot where less than two weeks before Judge Slattery had also lain.

Accompanied by Alice and the girls, Leora was in an end pew. The house doctor, the professor, and all of Mother Rosenbloom's employees were opposite them.

While Mass was being said, Leora was lost in wonder. She again saw the tree upon which coffins grew. Again the lid of one flew open and her mother stepped out.

She tried to fathom why the judge had died, and why Mother Rosenbloom had followed him. She asked herself,—why had Mother carried him into the rain? She could still see the mighty woman, with the handsome dead man thrown over her shoulder. She could feel the floor shake as Mother Rosenbloom walked with her burden.

Father Gilligan, who had given Mother Rosenbloom extreme unction, threw a spray of Holy Water over her.

A censor, in the hands of an altar boy, filled the church with incense.

Leora gazed at the pictures of Christ's journey to the cross and beyond, then closed her eyes as the choir sang the haunting AVE MARIA.

Father Gilligan began talking—

"Our Holy Mother Church is the roof of God, under which there is room for all. It acknowledges sin, and that its children are weak and erring. It covers alike the rich and the poor, and the murderer and the thief, with the purple of its understanding charity.

"We walk in the sunlight of God's love, holding out our hands to the cripple and the beggar, and the worn, and the heavy of heart.

"While men try to fathom mysteries, we accept them—for the mystery of the human heart is greater than all.

"It is my conviction, and that of the Holy Mother Church, that Jesus Christ is our Saviour, that He died to make us free—and like the rain from Heaven, His mercy falls on all.

"To follow the precepts of the Holy Mother Church is to walk in the resplendent shadow of God; and, though, we, like children, stumble and fall, He does not walk away from us, but helps us to rise and go forward, praising His name."

The altar boy stepped nearer to the coffin with the censer, while Father Gilligan continued,

"She who lies here did not desert us, though married in an alien creed. She kept in pure vigor the flower of her womanhood, and died in the one true faith."

The priest's voice rose, "She has gone to a land that is fairer than gold. She walks the golden streets arm-in-arm with Jesus.

"All that she has loved and lost are there to meet her.

"The great being who lay here but a few days ago in the majestic zenith of his manhood will be there." Leora covered her eyes. Alice put a hand on her arm. "There can be no death for such a man. If such a thing could be we are less than the dust, and not the immortal children of a thrice immortal Father." Leora sobbed.

"For them that are gone, we should not mourn—they are the vanguard of our glory—the forerunners of the Life Everlasting."

The light from the stained glass windows fell softly on Mother Rosenbloom while the priest stepped nearer to her.

"There is now no condemnation to them that are in Christ Jesus. For the law of the Spirit of life is Christ Jesus. And she now walks on the right hand of God, the Father, among His blessed saints. For the law of the Spirit of Life in Christ Jesus made her free of the Law of the Spirit of Death.

"The Spirit Himself beareth witness that we are children of God, and being His children, we are equal heirs to the Kingdom of God. Our sleeping sister here has but gone before us to lead the way to the most priceless mansions in His Kingdom.

"Her life among us was but a silent preparation for the life to come. She filled her days and nights with good deeds, as is testified by all of us who are here to do her honor."

He looked about the church for a moment, and resumed,

"For His sake we are killed all the day long. We are but sheep for His divine slaughter. But we are more than the children of God. We are conquerors through Him that loves us. For I am persuaded that neither death, nor life, nor angels, nor principalities, nor things present, nor things to come, nor powers, nor height, nor depth, nor any other creature, shall be able to separate us from the Love of God, which is in Christ Jesus, our Lord."

The sermon finished, the priest again threw Holy Water over Mother Rosenbloom, and muttered words in Latin. Raising his hands, he blessed the congregation, which soon marched in single file by Mother Rosenbloom's coffin.

A card was handed to each person.

A picture of Jesus Christ trimmed in black, a crown of thorns on his head, his hair falling to his shoulders, a cloak open to his waistline, a rope binding his upper arms, and his hands tied together, was on one side of the card. Beneath the picture of Christ were the words, ECCO HOMO. Beneath these words was,

My sweetest Jesus, be not my judge, but my Saviour.
(50 Days' Indulgence.)

On the other side of the card was printed,

Blessed are they that mourn, for they
shall be comforted. St. Matt. V. 4.

May Jesus have mercy on the Soul of

MARGARET ROSENBLOOM
(née Murphy)

Born December 23, 1876, Ireland.
Departed this life Saturday, August 12, 1932,
2:00 p.m. at _____.

Funeral services at St. Patrick's Church, Wednesday morning, August 16. Requiem High Mass at 9 o'clock, Rev. Father Henry Gilligan officiating.

O Gentlest heart of Jesus, ever present in the Blessed Sacrament, ever consumed with burning love for the poor captive souls in Purgatory have mercy on the soul of Thy departed servant.
Be not severe in Thy judgment but let some drops of Thy Precious

Blood fall upon the devouring flames, and do Thou, o merciful Saviour, send Thy angels to conduct her to a place of refreshment, light and peace.
    Amen.

Many waiting vehicles were outside the church.

In slow procession they followed Mother Rosenbloom to her grave.

Chapter 33

Like lost children, all returned to the desolate house. When lunch was served, they seated themselves about the table and ate sparingly.

The housekeeper's eyes were red. Otherwise she was frigid as ever.

"We'll have no more men here," she said.

"That's right," said the musician.

"I'm sick of seeing them," declared the housekeeper. "It's a wonder where they all come from—like so many rabbits."

"Well, Mother didn't mind," put in Selma.

"We'll go a long ways," said the old musician, "before we find a better place than this,—it's just like the sun's gone out."

"But didn't she have a nice funeral?" added Doris. "Yes," said the house doctor, "she'd of enjoyed that." "We'll all have to find new places now," decided

Selma, "it's like leaving home for me."

"None of us will starve right away," the housekeeper added. "No person in the house has been left less than five hundred dollars cash. Some have been left more." She looked at the professor, and Leora, and added, "so the secretary told me." No one else spoke of money.

The words came slowly, "Mother wouldn't forget." The old musician looked at his plate.

The personality of the barrel-built woman lingered everywhere in the house. In every room was an echo of the woman who had gone.

According to her last wish, her diamonds had been buried with her.

"She won't need them," said the house doctor, "the worms'll be too blind to see them."

"Maybe the ghouls won't," declared the housekeeper.

"They'd have to kill Mother over again," retorted the musician, "if they ever tried to steal her diamonds."

"She looked nice though," sighed the housekeeper more softly, "holding her watch the way she did—she looked just like she was asleep."

"Well, she is," blurted the house doctor, "and all hell can't wake her."

"Maybe that's not so bad—being through with clap doctors forever is worth something." Though the housekeeper's tone was sharp, the house doctor laughed.

"You will have your little joke at us doctors, won't you, Matilda?" he chuckled; "it was not Mother who needed my services."

"Well it wasn't me, either," snapped the housekeeper. "You know best," soothed the heavy man; "I've never examined you."

All laughed. The housekeeper rose indignantly, and left the table.

When the echo of her footsteps could no longer be heard, the doctor's eyes circled the table.

"A peculiar form of psychosis," he began.

"Speak English, for Christ's sake," stabbed Selma.

The doctor's little eyes opened wide as possible. "I can furnish knowledge but not brains," he said. The housekeeper stood in the doorway.

"It's no time to speak of either," she said. "Mother's just getting settled in her grave, and everybody's quarrelling already."

The words came, sharp as broken glass. She looked at the house doctor, "And I'll thank you for no more names." She left the dining-room again.

"Strange, isn't it?" The professor looked at the doctor. "If Mother were at the table, she'd be meek as a lamb."

"It can all be explained," vouched the doctor: "Certain functions undeveloped." He looked warily toward the door.

"Does she need a man?" asked Mary Ellen. "Succinctly, yes."

The housekeeper was again at the door. "As I was saying," resumed the doctor, "Mother Rosenbloom made a valiant fight. It was her time to go. Her work on earth was done. Men who delve into the higher mysteries are firmly of the opinion that, high or low, poor or rich, each has his work to do—when we are whisked away like thieves in the night to become angels in another sphere."

Selma tittered. "Imagine Mother an angel," she said.

The housekeeper had been listening intently to the doctor. She turned her stern eyes upon Selma.

"How can you make light of your dead benefactor?" she asked. "Didn't she give you a home and a chance to make a living and plenty of money?"

Selma scanned the housekeeper with defiant eyes. "Listen, old crowbait," she sneered, "I've had enough of this. Mother Rosenbloom don't owe me anything, and I don't owe her anything; if us girls hadn't gone to bed with every son-of-a-bitch that had ten dollars, where the hell would you have been?"

Leora put her hand on Selma's arm. The girl continued to look at the housekeeper, "Why the hell didn't you go to bed with somebody—you're so God-damned smart!"

"Dear, dear," said the doctor, "this is a high-class house."

When the laughter stopped, the housekeeper snapped, "I'm a lady and I refuse to answer."

"And I'm a whore," flared Selma, "and I want you to act like a lady." She looked from Leora to the other girls. "You'll never see the day in your damned cranky life you'll be the lady these girls are."

The housekeeper stood erect, her lips tight. "But I respect the dead," her words grated.

"Yes, you respect the dead—you'd better. You didn't respect Mother when she was alive, and us kids did—we played square—fifty-fifty, and you had a bone in your throat, spying on us every chance you got."

The housekeeper hissed, "You're a liar and a whore."

The words were hardly uttered when Leora threw a hard bun. It crashed against the housekeeper's lips. She was still off balance when Leora stood before her.

"Don't call any of us whores, you old witch." She slapped the housekeeper several times before Alice and Selma could intervene.

With bleeding lips, the housekeeper ran from the room.

Selma put an arm about the defiant Leora, and smiling, said, "You little tiger."

Leora straightened her hair before she said, "The damned hypocrite—she feels better than us in her heart, and I don't like it."

The doctor lifted his ponderous weight from the chair and looked at Leora, "What a wild and beautiful country you are to hear from," he remarked.

Selma, with her arm still around Leora, said, "Come, Leora, let's leave the house."

"Not me," returned Leora, "Mother left us some cash. No one's going to chase me away till I get it."

"The secretary will soon be here," said the professor. "It's all ready. I know that."

Jim Tully   159

"How do you know it?" asked Mary Ellen.

"It was the last thing Mother told me—she didn't want anyone to wait—she hated wills," the professor answered.

When the secretary came, all the girls were called into her small private room.

With solemn mien she gave each girl five hundred cash. "I've been asked to give this quickly," she said, "and Mother will sleep better out there if she knows I've obeyed her."

"Will you girls have dinner with me tonight?" the doctor asked as they returned from the secretary, "just a little farewell party. The professor is coming."

The girls looked at each other. "All right, Doctor," said Leora. "Where'll we meet you—I want to bring Alice."

The doctor studied. "Make it the Vanderhoff—eight o'clock."

He had gone but a few minutes when the doorbell rang noisily. The maid admitted several men. "Where's Mother?" one asked. Selma appeared, "She's dead—buried today."

"My God," exclaimed the man who had asked. Leora and Mary Ellen came into the room.

"Are you girls all packed?" asked Selma.

"Yes," Leora answered.

The old professor thumbed the piano keys as if in a daze.

The men looked about helplessly. Finally one said, "Well, let's have a drink to Mother's memory." "It's all right with us," returned Selma.

A bottle of wine was brought. Just as the glasses were lifted, the housekeeper entered and looked askance.

"Well," said the first speaker, as they left, "we'll be seein' you."

Their car could be heard starting.

"Let's get our things out of here," suggested Selma, going to the telephone.

"All right," the other girls agreed.

With baggage on the way to the railroad station, they bade farewell to the maids and the cook, then went in a body to the housekeeper.

"We don't like each other," said Selma, "but let's be nice for Mother's sake."

"I'll forgive you," she said to Selma; then looking sternly at Leora, "but not you." She felt her swollen lips.

"All right then," said Leora, "I'll forgive you."

Without looking back at the house in which they had experienced so much, the girls hurried away with the professor.

Selma became thoughtful.

"It's our last day together," she said, "I'm taking a boat down the river tomorrow."

"Gee, that would be fun," said Doris.

"Why don't you go along?" suggested Selma. "Business is good in New Orleans."

"Why sure, I may as well be there as any place," decided Doris.

"We can get the boat out of Davenport tomorrow." Selma paused before saying, "I used to live near Clinton."

For a second she thought of a vagabond boy and a turtle. To banish them she began to hum,

> It's the wrong way to diddle Mary,
> It's the wrong way, I know,
> It's the wrong, wrong, way to diddle Mary,
> By God, I know.

Breaking off her humming, she asked Mary Ellen, "What are you going to do, Mary?"

Mary Ellen turned to Leora. "Shall I tell her?" she asked.

"Certainly," said Leora.

"I'm going to be married."

"Well, I'll be damned," snapped Selma. "You've been holding out on us."

"And you, Leora?" The girls and the professor looked at her.

"I'm going to be married too."

All looked at Leora in surprise.

"I thought you loved Judge Slattery," said Selma. "I did."

It was some time before Leora spoke again. "We ought to remember June," she said. "Let's send her something."

"Mother remembered her," muttered the professor. "Are you sure?" asked Mary Ellen.

"Yes, because I've been taking her money every week —besides, Mother told me."

The doctor, bulging in his evening clothes, was waiting for them.

They had touched the high notes of life together. It was now difficult to keep their thoughts from wandering.

After the doctor had ordered with extreme dignity, Selma blurted, "What do you think of that damn housekeeper—she'd starve to death in a ten cent house, and yet she ordered women like us around."

"Tut-tut," urged the doctor.

"Tut yourself," returned Selma.

All were relieved when the dinner at last broke up.

The professor held Leora's hand long in parting. Mary Ellen sobbed in kissing her good-bye. She was taunted by Selma who had tears in her eyes.

The doctor and Leora accompanied Alice to her apartment.

"Now don't you girls lose me in the shuffle," he said in parting.

"We won't, Doctor, we may need you," laughed Alice.

A silence came between the girls after the doctor had gone. It was broken by Leora, "It's terrible to go back and marry him after—" She did not finish.

"Oh, well," returned Alice, "you may learn to love him—men are all alike anyhow."

"You know better, Alice." For a second Leora had the impulse to confide her secret to Alice. Then she suddenly decided to keep it to herself forever.

Leora's heart was low. To cheer her, Alice clapped her hands and said, "Let's telephone the doctor." "All right," agreed Leora.

"Tell him you're leaving right away to marry him." "All right," again agreed Leora.

When Leora waved from the observation car that evening, Alice said, "Give Mother and all my love and tell them I'll be home for a visit this summer." "I will," said Leora.

Leora went to her seat and gazed out of the window. Smiling vaguely, she thought of Mrs. Haley. Her eyes closed. Tomorrow she would be Mrs. Jonas Farway. And she would bring her husband another man's child.

She thought a long time, then shrugged her shoulders,

"It's mine anyhow—and *his*."

Again she gazed out of the window.

Made in the USA
Lexington, KY
29 December 2013